MACABRE MILITARY STORIES

Also by Ronald Holmes

WITCHCRAFT IN BRITISH HISTORY
THE LEGEND OF SAWNEY BEAN

MACABRE MILITARY STORIES

Compiled and edited by

RONALD HOLMES

LEO COOPER   LONDON

For
Jessie, Lillian and Maisie

First Published in Great Britain in 1979 by
LEO COOPER LTD
196 Shaftesbury Avenue, London WC2H 8JL

Copyright © 1979 by Ronald Holmes

ISBN 0 85052 244 7

Set in 10 on 13 pt Times
Printed in Great Britain by
Clarke, Doble & Brendon Ltd
at Plymouth and London

CONTENTS

v

ACKNOWLEDGEMENTS

The editor wishes to thank Miss Avril Skupski for assistance with this work and the following authors, or their executors or agents, and publishers for permission to include copyright material in this book:

The estate of the late Arthur Machen: *The Soldiers' Rest*; Mrs Rose Elton and Chatto & Windus: *A Trade Report Only*; Scott Meredith Literary Agency, Inc: *The Living Dead*; Miss Barbara Softly: *Master Ghost and I*; J. M. Dent & Sons Ltd: *The Roll-Call of the Reef*; Ed Victor Ltd: *The Scarlet King*; A. D. Peters & Co Ltd: *The Battle*.

Every effort has been made to trace the copyright holders of these stories. The editor offers his apologies in the event of any necessary acknowledgement being accidentally omitted.

INTRODUCTION

As its name implies, this anthology of ghost stories is about military men and is intended to be read by military men or those, like myself, who are interested in military matters, although each story stands alone as one which will please the most discerning reader of tales of the macabre.

The idea that a work of this sort could and should be produced occurred to me many years ago when reading *A Watcher by the Dead*, written by the eccentric American author Ambrose Bierce. Three physicians discuss the fear of the dead and one asserts that it 'is hereditary and incurable' and continues . . . 'Oh, but it is "in the system" for all that, it needs only the right conditions – what Shakespeare calls the "confederate season" – to manifest itself in some very disagreeable way that will open your eyes. Physicians and soldiers are, of course, more nearly free from it than others.'

Why, I asked myself, should soldiers be considered to be free from awareness of, or denied access to, the spirits of the departed? It is certainly a widely-held belief. The spirits themselves do not seem to have such inhibitions regarding soldiers and, from my experience, seem to contact, when they wish, people from any walk of life. Quite recently I have been made aware of an incident which concerned a British married quarter near the town of Fallingbostel in Germany where the young daughter of the family spent many hours happily playing with the spirit of a young German girl.

In answer to this question I can only point out that during the classical period of the ghost and horror story it was usual for the principal character to be at least neurotic if not outright demented. Such were the characters featured in the stories of Sheridan Le Fanu and Edgar Allan Poe, and more recently H. P. Lovercraft created a whole population who reacted individually and collectively to the effects of severe in-breeding and all that that implies. There was nothing to be found in common with these fictitious characters and military men in general and that particular period saw practically no ghost stories in which soldiers were involved.

However, before and after that time authors had no such limitations and although such stories were rare there were enough to provide many interesting hours of research. In selecting the stories in this collection I have discarded those which have a mere flavour of the military – stories which contain a principal character with a military rank but where the action could have occurred to a banker or a pianist. The soldiers you will meet in this book, with few exceptions, wear dirty uniforms and have known what it is to be under fire.

Every story in this collection gives a different approach to the situation where a soldier must face up to the supernatural and yet full allowance is made for the differing personalities that soldiers have and how they might respond to different situations. *The Bold Dragoon* depicts the hard-living, hard-swearing fellow and his reactions to the midnight happenings in a haunted inn, while the ship-wrecked trumpeter in *The Roll-Call of the Reef* is driven to distraction by the loss of his comrades. And yet there is also room for humour, for this too is part of life – and death.

I have also selected the stories with an eye to authentic details of the military scene and have tried to represent the main theatres of military activity in which British or European troops have been engaged over the past 300 years—with an excursion into the future. Although there have been ghost stories about military leaders since the earliest times – even before the ghost of Caesar appeared to Brutus to warn him of his death at the Battle of Philippi – there have been few items of fiction worthy of inclusion written before the eighteenth century and the American Wars of Independence somehow has never fired the imaginations of ghost writers. *The Phantom Regiment* is reprinted here for the first time since 1847 and is a classic piece of writing, while two true ghostly incidents from the War of Independence are included (reprinted in full for the first time) for completeness.

The past three centuries have involved British and European troops in civil war, invasion, colonization and conquest and it is hoped that the stories in this collection cover the whole field.

But what of the ghosts? The ghosts are just as varied in their own way. There are ghosts of the past, present and future; ghosts singly and in regiments; ghosts in truth and fiction; ghostly marines and infantrymen; witches and vampires; all included in stories by British and American authors of the highest calibre.

RONALD HOLMES

Wetherby, Yorkshire

WASHINGTON IRVING

Washington Irving (1783–1859) will probably be long remembered for *The Legend of Sleepy Hollow* which was brought to the screen a few years ago by Disney aided by the voice of Bing Crosby. It told of the terror-stricken schoolteacher, Ichabod, who was pursued through the night by a headless horseman. He held a Staff Colonelcy during the War of 1812 (sometimes called the Second War of Independence) when the United States declared war on Britain and invaded Canada.

After three years travel in Europe where he met and was encouraged to write by Sir Walter Scott he returned to America to continue his literary career. He was soon to be acclaimed as the 'inventor of the short story' and the majority of his works showed his interest in the Dutch, his delightful humour and predilection for the macabre.

The intrepid hero of *The Bold Dragoon* is the very antithesis of a trembling schoolmaster but Irving describes his adventures with the same wry humour as those of Ichabod.

1 · THE BOLD DRAGOON

My grandfather was a bold dragoon, for it's a profession, d'ye see, that has run in the family. All my forefathers have been dragoons, and died on the field of honour, except myself, and I hope my posterity may be able to say the same; however, I don't mean to be vain glorious. Well, my grandfather, as I said, was a bold dragoon, and had served in the Low Countries. In fact, he was one of that very army, which, according to my uncle Toby, swore so terribly in Flanders. He could swear a good stick himself; and moreover was the very man that introduced the doctrine Corporal Trim mentions of radical heat and radical moisture; or, in other words, the mode of keeping out the damps of ditch-water by burnt brandy. Be that as it may, it's nothing to the purport of my story. I only tell it to show you that my grandfather was a man not easily to be humbugged. He had seen service, or, according to his own phrase, he had seen the devil – and that's saying everything.

Well, gentlemen, my grandfather was on his way to England, for which he intended to embark from Ostend – bad luck to the place: for one where I was kept by storms and head winds for three long days, and the devil of a jolly companion or pretty face to comfort me. Well, as I was saying, my grandfather was on his way to England, or rather to Ostend – no matter which, it's all the same. So one evening, towards nightfall, he rode jollily into Bruges. Very like you all know Bruges, gentlemen; a queer old-fashioned Flemish town, once, they say, a great place for trade and money-making in old times, when the Mynheers were in their glory; but almost as large and as empty as an Irishman's pocket at the present day. Well, gentlemen, it was at the time of the annual fair. All Bruges was crowded; and the canals swarmed with Dutch boats, and the streets swarmed with Dutch merchants; and there was hardly any getting along for goods, wares, and merchandises, and peasants in big breeches, and women in half a score of petticoats.

My grandfather rode jollily along, in his easy slashing way, for he was a saucy sun shiny fellow – staring about him at the motley crowd, and the old houses with gable ends to the street, and storks' nests on the chimneys; winking at the yafrows who showed their faces at the windows, and joking the women right and left in the street; all of whom laughed, and took it in amazing good part; for though he did not know a word of the language, yet he had always a knack of making himself understood among the women.

Well, gentlemen, it being the time of the annual fair, all the town was crowded, every inn and tavern full, and my grandfather applied in vain from one to the other for admittance. At length he rode up to an old rickety inn that looked ready to fall to pieces, and which all the rats would have run away from, if they could have found room in any other house to put their heads. It was just such a queer building as you see in Dutch pictures, with a tall roof that reached up into the clouds, and as many garrets one over the other, as the seven heavens of Mahomet. Nothing had saved it from tumbling down but a stork's nest on the chimney, which always brings good luck to a house in the Low Countries; and at the very time of my grandfather's arrival there were two of these long-legged birds of grace standing like ghosts on the chimney top. Faith, but they've kept the house on its legs to this very day, for you may see it any time you pass through Bruges, as it stands there yet, only it is turned into a brewery of strong Flemish beer; at least it was so when I came that way after the battle of Waterloo.

My grandfather eyed the house curiously as he approached. It might not have altogether struck his fancy, had he not seen in large letters over the door,

HEER VERKOOPT MAN GOEDEN DRANK

My grandfather had learnt enough of the language to know that the sign promised good liquor. 'This is the house for me,' said he, stopping short before the door.

The sudden appearance of a dashing dragoon was an event in an old inn, frequented only by the peaceful sons of traffic. A rich burgher of Antwerp, a stately ample man in a broad Flemish hat, and who was the great man, and great patron of the establishment, sat smoking a clean long pipe on one side of the door; a fat little distiller of Geneva, from Schiedam, sat smoking on the other; and the bottle-nosed host stood in the door, and the comely hostess, in crimped cap, beside him; and the hostess's daughter, a plump Flanders lass, with long gold pendants in her ears, was at a side window.

'Humph!' said the rich burgher of Antwerp, with a sulky glance at the stranger.

'*Der duyvel!*' said the fat little distiller of Schiedam.

The landlord saw, with the quick glance of a publican, that the new guest was not at all, at all to the taste of the old ones; and, to tell the truth, he did not himself like my grandfather's saucy eye. He shook his head. 'Not a garret in the house but was full.'

'Not a garret!' echoed the landlady.

'Not a garret!' echoed the daughter.

The burgher of Antwerp, and the little distiller of Schiedam, continued to smoke their pipes sullenly, eyeing the enemy askance from under their broad hats, but said nothing.

My grandfather was not a man to be brow-beaten. He threw the reins on his horse's neck, cocked his head on one side, stuck one arm akimbo, 'Faith and troth!' said he, 'but I'll sleep in this house this very night.' As he said this he gave a slap on his thigh, by way of emphasis – the slap went to the landlady's heart.

He followed up the vow by jumping off his horse, and making his way past the staring Mynheers into the public room. Maybe you've been in the bar-room of an old Flemish inn – faith, but a handsome chamber it was as you'd wish to see; with a brick floor, and a great fire-place, with the whole

Bible history in glazed tiles; and then the mantel-piece, pitching itself head foremost out of the wall, with a whole regiment of cracked teapots and earthen jugs paraded on it; not to mention half a dozen great Delft platters, hung about the room by way of pictures; and the little bar in one corner, and the bouncing barmaid inside of it, with a red calico cap and yellow ear-drops.

My grandfather snapped his fingers over his head, as he cast an eye round the room. 'Faith this is the very house I've been looking after,' said he.

There was some further show of resistance on the part of the garrison; but my grandfather was an old soldier, and an Irishman to boot, and not easily repulsed, especially after he had got into the fortress. So he blarneyed the landlord, kissed the landlord's wife, tickled the landlord's daughter, chucked the bar-maid under the chin; and it was agreed on all hands that it would be a thousand pities, and a burning shame into the bargain, to turn such a bold dragoon into the streets. So they laid their heads together, that is to say, my grandfather and the landlady, and it was at length agreed to accommodate him with an old chamber that had been for some time shut up.

'Some say it's haunted,' whispered the landlady's daughter; 'but you are a bold dragoon, and I dare say don't fear ghosts.'

'The divil a bit!' said my grandfather, pinching her plump cheek. 'But if I should be troubled by ghosts, I've been to the Red Sea in my time, and have a pleasant way of laying them, my darling.'

And then he whispered something to the girl which made her laugh, and give him a good-humoured box on the ear. In short, there was nobody knew better how to make his way among the petticoats than my grandfather.

In a little while, as was his usual way, he took complete possession of the house, swaggering all over it; into the stable to look after his horse, into the kitchen to look after his supper. He had something to say or do with every one; smoked with the Dutchmen, drank with the Germans, slapped the landlord on the shoulder, romped with his daughter and the bar-maid: never since the days of Alley Croaker had such a rattling blade been seen. The landlord stared at him with astonishment; the landlord's daughter hung her head and giggled whenever he came near; and as he swaggered along the corridor, with his sword trailing by his side, the maids looked after him, and whispered to one another, 'What a proper man!'

At supper, my grandfather took command of the table-d'hote as though he had been at home; helped everybody, not forgetting himself; talked with every one, whether he understood their language or not; and made his way into the intimacy of the rich burgher of Antwerp, who had never been known to be sociable with anyone during his life. In fact, he revolutionized the whole establishment, and gave it such a rouse that the very house reeled with it. He outsat everyone at table excepting the little fat distiller of Schiedam, who sat soaking a long time before he broke forth; but when he did, he was a very devil incarnate. He took a violent affection for my grandfather; so they sat drinking and smoking, and telling stories, and singing Dutch and Irish songs, without understanding a word each other said, until the little Hollander was fairly swamped with his own gin and water, and carried off to bed, whooping and hiccuping, and trolling the burthen of a low Dutch love song.

Well, gentlemen, my grandfather was shown to his quarters up a large staircase, composed of loads of hewn timber; and through long rigmarole passages, hung with blackened paintings of fish, and fruit, and game and country frolics, and huge kitchens, and portly Burgomasters, such as you see about old-fashioned Flemish inns, till at length he arrived at his room.

An old-times chamber it was, sure enough, and crowded with all kinds of trumpery. It looked like an infirmary for decayed and superannuated furniture, where every thing diseased or disabled was sent to nurse or to be forgotten. Or rather it might be taken for a general congress of old legitimate moveables, where every king and country had a representative. No two chairs were alike. Such high backs and low backs, and leather bottoms, and worsted bottoms, and straw bottoms, and no bottoms; and cracked marble tables with curiously-carved legs, holding balls in their claws, as though they were going to play at nine-pins.

My grandfather made a bow to the motley assemblage as he entered, and, having undressed himself, placed his light in the fire-place, asking pardon of the tongs, which seemed to be making love to the shovel in the chimney corner, and whispering soft nonsense in its ear.

The rest of the guests were by this time sound asleep, for your Mynheers are huge sleepers. The house-maids, one by one, crept up yawning to their attics, and not a female head in the inn was laid on a pillow that night without dreaming of the bold dragoon.

B

My grandfather, for his part, got into bed, and drew over him one of those great bags of down, under which they smother a man of the Low Countries; and there he lay, melting between two feather beds, like an anchovy sandwich between two slices of toast and butter. He was a warm-complexioned man, and this smothering played the very deuce with him. So, sure enough, in a little time it seemed as if a legion of imps were twitching at him, and all the blood in his veins was in a fever heat.

He lay still, however, until all the house was quiet, excepting the snoring Mynheers from the different chambers; who answered one another in all kinds of tones and cadences, like so many bullfrogs in a swamp. The quieter the house became, the more unquiet became my grandfather. He waxed warmer and warmer, until at length the bed became too hot to hold him.

'Faith, there's no standing this any longer,' says he. So he jumped out of bed, and went strolling about the house.

Well, my grandfather had been for some time absent from his room, and was returning perfectly cool, when just as he reached the door he heard a strange noise within. He paused and listened. It seemed as if someone were trying to hum a tune in defiance of the asthma. He recollected the report of the room being haunted; but he was no believer in ghosts, so he pushed the door gently open and peeped in.

Egad, gentlemen, there was a gambol carrying on within enough to have astonished St Anthony himself. By the light of the fire he saw a pale, weazen-faced fellow in a long flannel gown and a tall white night-cap with a tassel to it, who sat by the fire with a bellows under his arm by way of bagpipe, from which he forced the asthmatical music that had bothered my grandfather. As he played, too, he kept twitching about with a thousand queer contortions, nodding his head, and bobbing about his tasselled night-cap.

My grandfather thought this very odd and mighty presumptuous, and was about to demand what business he had to play his wind instrument in another gentleman's quarters, when a new cause of astonishment met his eye. From the opposite side of the room a long-backed, bandy-legged chair, covered with leather, and studded all over in a coxcombical fashion with little brass nails, got suddenly into motion, thrust out first a claw foot, then a crooked arm, and at length, making a leg, slided gracefully up to an easy chair of tarnished brocade, with a hole in its bottom, and led it gallantly out in a ghostly minuet about the floor.

The musician now played fiercer and fiercer, and bobbed his head and his night-cap about like mad. By degrees the dancing mania seemed to seize upon all the other pieces of furniture. The antique, long-bodied chairs paired off in couples and led down a country dance; a three-legged stool danced a hornpipe, though horribly puzzled by its supernumerary leg; while the amorous tongs seized the shovel round the waist, and whirled it about the room in a German waltz. In short, all the movables got in motion; pirouetting, hands across, right and left, like so many devils: all except a great clothes-press, which kept curtseying and curtseying, in a corner, like a dowager, in exquisite time to the music; being rather too corpulent to dance, or perhaps at a loss for a partner.

My grandfather concluded the latter to be the reason; so being, like a true Irishman, devoted to the sex, and at all times ready for a frolic, he bounced into the room, called to the musician to strike up Paddy O'Rafferty, capered up to the clothes-press, and seized upon two handles to lead her out; – when – whirr! the whole revel was at an end. The chairs, tables, tongs, and shovel slunk in an instant as quietly into their places as if nothing had happened, and the musician vanished up the chimney, leaving the bellows behind him in his hurry. My grandfather found himself seated in the middle of the floor with the clothes-press sprawling before him, and the two handles jerked off, and in his hands.

Well, gentlemen, as the clothes-press was a mighty heavy body, and my grandfather likewise, particularly in rear, you may easily suppose that two such heavy bodies coming to the ground would make a bit of a noise. Faith, the old mansion shook as though it had mistaken it for an earthquake. The whole garrison was alarmed. The landlord, who slept below, hurried up with a candle to inquire the cause, but with all his haste his daughter had hurried to the scene of uproar before him. The landlord was followed by the landlady, who was followed by the bouncing bar-maid, who was followed by the simpering chambermaids, all holding together, as well as they could, such garments as they had first lain hands on; but all in a terrible hurry to see what the deuce was to pay in the chamber of the bold Dragoon.

My grandfather related the marvellous scene he had witnessed, and the broken handles of the prostrate clothes-press bore testimony to the fact. There was no contesting such evidence; particularly with a lad of my grandfather's complexion, who seemed able to make good every word

either with sword or shillelah. So the landlord scratched his head and
looked silly, as he was apt to do when puzzled. The landlady scratched –
no, she did not scratch her head, but she knit her brow, and did not seem
half pleased with the explanation. But the landlady's daughter corroborated it by recollecting that the last person who had dwelt in that
chamber was a famous juggler who had died of St Vitus's dance, and had
no doubt infected all the furniture.

This set all things to rights, particularly when the chamber-maids
declared that they had all witnessed strange carryings on in that room; and
as they declared this 'upon their honours', there could not remain a doubt
upon the subject.

Where my grandfather passed the rest of the night was a secret he never
disclosed and it was not a subject we cared to raise lightly.

Was it all just a dream, you might well ask? Faith, but I should have
liked to see any man tell my grandfather that!

SIR A. QUILLER-COUCH

The Napoleonic Wars saw frenzied military activity all along the south coast of England. Invasion from France was expected at one time and a chain of Martello Towers were built to protect the coast. After Trafalgar there was a constant traffic of ships laiden with men and supplies for the British armies in Spain from all the main ports along the English Channel. Not all of them survived the journey across the Bay of Biscay and some, as here related, went aground on the inhospitable Cornish coast.

Sir Arthur Thomas Quiller-Couch (1863–1944) was an English Scholar and man of letters who also wrote under 'Q'. He was in every way a Cornishman who loved his country and it flavoured all his works. In *The Roll-Call of the Reef* he describes the wreck of a troop-ship with rare realism as well as the eerie events which followed.

2 · THE ROLL-CALL OF THE REEF

'Yes, sir,' said my host the quarryman, reaching down the relics from their hook in the wall over the chimney-piece; 'they've hung there all my time, and most of my father's. The women won't touch 'em; they're afraid of the story. So here they'll dangle, and gather dust and smoke, till another tenant comes and tosses 'em out o' doors for rubbish. Whew! 'tis coarse weather.'

He went to the door, opened it, and stood studying the gale that beat upon his cottage-front, straight from the Manacle Reef. The rain drove past him into the kitchen, aslant like threads of gold silk in the shine of the wreckwood fire. Meanwhile by the same firelight I examined the relics on my knee. The metal of each was tarnished out of knowledge. But the trumpet was evidently an old cavalry trumpet, and the threads of its part-coloured sling, though frayed and dusty, still hung together. Around the side-drum, beneath its cracked brown varnish, I could hardly trace a royal coat-of-arms, and a legend running -- *Per Mare per Terram* – the motto of the Marines. Its parchment, though coloured and scented with wood-

11

smoke, was limp and mildewed; and I began to tighten up the straps –
under which the drumsticks had been loosely thrust – with the idle purpose
of trying if some music might be got out of the old drum yet.

But as I turned it on my knee, I found the drum attached to the trumpet-
sling by a curious barrel-shaped padlock, and paused to examine this. The
body of the lock was composed of half a dozen brass rings, set accurately
edge to edge; and, rubbing the brass with my thumb, I saw that each of
the six had a series of letters engraved around it.

I knew the trick of it, I thought. Here was one of those word-padlocks,
once so common; only to be opened by getting the rings to spell a certain
word, which the dealer confides to you.

My host shut and barred the door, and came back to the hearth.

'Twas just such a wind – east by south – that brought in what you've
got between your hands. Back in the year 'nine it was; my father has told
me the tale a score o' times. You're twisting round the rings, I see. But
you'll never guess the word. Parson Kendall, he made the word, and
locked down a couple of ghosts in their graves with it; and when his time
came, he went to his own grave and took the word with him.'

'Whose ghosts, Matthew?'

'You want the story, I see, sir. My father could tell it better than I can.
He was a young man in the year 'nine, unmarried at the time, and living
in this very cottage just as I be. That's how he came to get mixed up with
the tale.'

He took a chair, lit a short pipe, and unfolded the story in a low musing
voice, with his eyes fixed on the dancing violet flames.

'Yes, he'd ha' been about thirty year old in January of the year 'nine.
The storm got up in the night o' the twenty-first o' that month. My father
was dressed and out long before daylight; he never was one to 'bide in bed,
let be that the gale by this time was pretty near lifting the thatch over his
head. Besides which, he'd fenced a small 'taty-patch that winter, down by
Lowland Point, and he wanted to see if it stood the night's work. He took
the path across Gunner's Meadow – where they buried most of the bodies
afterwards. The wind was right in his teeth at the time, and once on the
way (he's told me this often) a great strip of oreweed came flying through
the darkness and fetched him a slap on the cheek like a cold hand. But he
made shift pretty well till he got to Lowland, and then had to drop upon
his hands and knees and crawl, digging his fingers every now and then into

the shingle to hold on, for he declared to me that the stones, some of them as big as a man's head, kept rolling and driving past till it seemed the whole foreshore was moving westward under him. The fence was gone, of course; not a stick left to show where it stood; so that, when first he came to the place, he thought he must have missed his bearings. My father, sir, was a very religious man; and if he reckoned the end of the world was at hand – there in the great wind and night, among the moving stones – you may believe he was certain of it when he heard a gun fired, and, with the same, saw a flame shoot up out of the darkness to windward, making a sudden fierce light in all the place about. All he could find to think or say was, "The Second Coming – The Second Coming! The Bridegroom cometh, and the wicked He will toss like a ball into a large country!" and being already upon his knees, he just bowed his head and 'bided, saying this over and over.

'But by'n-by, between two squalls, he made bold to lift his head and look, and then by the light – a bluish colour 'twas – he saw all the coast clear away to Manacle Point, and off the Manacles, in the thick of the weather, a sloop-of-war with top-gallants housed, driving stern foremost towards the reef. It was she, of course, that was burning the flare. My father could see the white streak and the ports of her quite plain as she rose to it, a little outside the breakers, and he guessed easy enough that her captain had just managed to wear ship, and was trying to force her nose to the sea with the help of her small bower anchor and the scrap or two of canvas that hadn't yet been blown out of her. But while he looked, she fell off, giving her broadside to it foot by foot, and drifting back on the breakers around Carn dû and the Varses. The rocks lie so thick there-abouts, that 'twas a toss up which she struck first; at any rate, my father couldn't tell at the time, for just then the flare died down and went out.

'Well, sir, he turned then in the dark and started back for Coverack to cry the dismal tidings – though well knowing the ship and crew to be past any hope; and as he turned, the wind lifted him and tossed him forward "like a ball", as he'd been saying, and homeward along the foreshore. As you know, 'tis ugly work, even by daylight, picking your way among the stones there, and my father was prettily knocked about at first in the dark. But by this 'twas nearer seven than six o'clock, and the day spreading. By the time he reached North Corner, a man could see to read print; hows'ever, he looked neither out to sea nor towards Coverack, but headed straight for the first cottage – the same that stands above North Corner today. A man named Billy Ede lived there then, and when my father burst into the kitchen bawling, "Wreck! wreck!" he saw Billy Ede's wife, Ann, standing there in her clogs, with a shawl over her head, and her clothes wringing wet.

' "Save the chap!" says Billy Ede's wife, Ann. "What d' 'ee mean by crying stale fish at that rate?"

' "But 'tis a wreck, I tell 'ee. I've a-zeed 'n!"

' "Why, so 'tis," says she, "and I've a-zeed 'n too; and so has everyone with an eye in his head."

'And with that she pointed straight over my father's shoulder, and he turned; and there, close under Dolor Point, at the end of Coverack town, he saw *another* wreck washing, and the point black with people, like emmets, running to and fro in the morning light. While he stood staring at her, he heard a trumpet sounded on board, the notes coming in little jerks, like a bird rising against the wind; but faintly, of course, because of the distance and the gale blowing – though this had dropped a little.

' "She's a transport," said Billy Ede's wife, Ann, "and full of horse soldiers, fine long men. When she struck they must ha' pitched the hosses over first to lighten the ship, for a score of dead hosses had washed in afore I left, half an hour back. An' three or four soldiers, too – fine long corpses in white breeches and jackets of blue and gold. I held the lantern to one. Such a straight young man!"

'My father asked her about the trumpeting.

' "That's the queerest bit of all. She was burnin' a light when me an' my man joined the crowd down there. All her masts had gone; whether they carried away, or were cut away to ease her, I don't rightly know. Anyway, there she lay 'pon the rocks with her decks bare. Her keelson was broke under her and her bottom sagged and stove, and she had just settled down like a sitting hen – just the leastest list to starboard; but a man could stand there easy. They had rigged up ropes across her, from bulwark to bulwark, an' beside these the men were mustered, holding on like grim death whenever the sea made a clean breach over them, an' standing up like heroes as soon as it passed. The captain an' the officers were clinging to the rail of the quarter-deck, all in their golden uniforms, waiting for the end as if 'twas King George they expected. There was no way to help, for she lay right beyond cast of line, though our folk tried it fifty times. And beside them clung a trumpeter, a whacking big man, an' between the heavy seas he would lift his trumpet with one hand, and blow a call; and every time he blew, the men gave a cheer. There" (she says) "– hark 'ee now – there he goes agen. But you won't hear no cheering any more, for few are left to cheer, and their voices weak. Bitter cold the wind is, and I reckon it numbs their grip o' the ropes, for they were dropping off fast with every sea when my man sent me home to get his breakfast. *Another* wreck, you say? Well, there's no hope for the tender dears, if 'tis the Manacles. You'd better run down and help yonder; though 'tis little help that any man can give. Not one came in alive while I was there. The tide's flowing, an' she won't hold together another hour, they say."

'Well, sure enough, the end was coming fast when my father got down to the point. Six men had been cast up alive, or just breathing – a seaman and five troopers. The seaman was the only one that had breath to speak; and while they were carrying him into the town, the word went round that the ship's name was the *Despatch*, transport, homeward bound from Corunna, with a detachment of the 7th Hussars, that had been fighting out there with Sir John Moore. The seas had rolled her farther over by this time, and given her decks a pretty sharp slope; but a dozen men still held on, seven by the ropes near the ship's waist, a couple near the break of the poop, and three on the quarter-deck. Of these three my father made out one to be the skipper; close by him clung an officer in full regimentals – his name, they heard after, was Captain Duncanfield; and last came the tall trumpeter; and if you'll believe me, the fellow was making shift there, at the very last, to blow *God Save the King*. What's more, he got to *"Send us victorious"* before an extra big sea came bursting across and washed them off the deck – every man but one of the pair beneath the poop – and *he* dropped his hold before the next wave; being stunned, I reckon. The others went out of sight at once, but the trumpeter – being, as I said, a powerful man as well as a tough swimmer – rose like a duck, rode out a couple of breakers, and came in on the crest of the third. The folks looked to see him broke like an egg at their feet; but when the smother cleared, there he was, lying face downward on a ledge below them; and one of the men that happened to have a rope round him – I forget the fellow's name, if I ever heard it – jumped down and grabbed him by the ankle as he began to slip back. Before the next big sea, the pair were hauled high enough to be out of harm, and another heave brought them up to grass. Quick work;

but master trumpeter wasn't quite dead; nothing worse than a cracked head and three staved ribs. In twenty minutes or so they had him in bed, with the doctor to tend him.

'Now was the time – nothing being left alive upon the transport – for my father to tell of the sloop he'd seen driving upon the Manacles. And when he got a hearing, though the most were set upon salvage, and believed a wreck in the hand, so to say, to be worth half a dozen they couldn't see, a good few volunteered to start off with him and have a look. They crossed Lowland Point; no ship to be seen on the Manacles, nor anywhere upon the sea. One or two was for calling my father a liar. "Wait till we come to Dean Point," said he. Sure enough, on the far side of Dean Point, they found the sloop's mainmast washing about with half a dozen men lashed to it – men in red jackets – every mother's son drowned and staring, and a little farther on, just under Dean, three or four bodies cast up on the shore, one of them a small drummer-boy, side-drum and all; and, near by, part of a ship's gig, with "H.M.S. *Primrose*" cut on the stern-board. From this point on, the shore was littered thick with wreckage and dead bodies – the most of them Marines in uniform; and in Godrey Cove, in particular, a heap of furniture from the captain's cabin, and amongst it a water-tight box, not much damaged, and full of papers; by which, when it came to be examined next day, the wreck was easily made out to be the *Primrose*, of eighteen guns, outward bound from Portsmouth, with a fleet of transports for the Spanish War – thirty sail, I've heard, but I've never heard what became of them. Being handled by merchant skippers, no doubt they rode out the gale and reached the Tagus safe and sound. Not but what the captain of the *Primrose* (Mein was his name) did quite right to try and club-haul his vessel when he found himself under the land: only he never ought to have got there if he took proper soundings. But it's easy talking.

'The *Primrose*, sir, was a handsome vessel – for her size, one of the handsomest in the King's service – and newly fitted out at Plymouth Dock. So the boys had brave pickings from her in the way of brass-work, ship's instruments, and the like, let alone some barrels of stores not much spoiled. They loaded themselves with as much as they could carry, and started for home, meaning to make a second journey before the preventive men got wind of their doings and came to spoil the fun. But as my father was passing back under the Dean, he happened to take a look over his shoulder at the bodies there. "Hullo," says he, and dropped his gear: "I do believe there's a leg moving!" And, running fore, he stooped over the small drummer-boy that I told you about. The poor little chap was lying there, with his face a mass of bruises and his eyes closed: but he had shifted one leg an inch or two, and was still breathing. So my father pulled out a knife and cut him free from his drum – that was lashed on to him with a double turn of Manilla rope – and took him up and carried him along here, to this very room that we're sitting in. He lost a good deal by this, for when he went back to fetch his bundle the preventive men had got hold of it, and were thick as thieves along the foreshore; so that 'twas only by paying one or two to look the other way that he picked up anything worth carrying off: which you'll allow to be hard, seeing that he was the first man to give news of the wreck.

'Well, the inquiry was held, of course, and my father gave evidence; and for the rest they had to trust to the sloop's papers: for not a soul was saved besides the drummer-boy, and he was raving in a fever, brought on by the cold and the fright. And the seaman and the five troopers gave evidence about the loss of the *Despatch*. The tall trumpeter, too, whose ribs were healing, came forward and kissed the Book; but somehow his head had been hurt in coming ashore, and he talked foolish-like, and 'twas easy seen he would never be a proper man again. The others were taken up to Plymouth, and so went their ways; but the trumpeter stayed on in Coverack; and King George, finding he was fit for nothing, sent him down a trifle of a pension after a while – enough to keep him in board and lodging, with a bit of tobacco over.

'Now the first time that this man – William Tallifer, he called himself – met with the drummer-boy, was about a fortnight after the little chap had bettered enough to be allowed a short walk out of doors, which he took, if you please, in full regimentals. There never was a soldier so proud of his dress. His own suit had shrunk a brave bit with the salt water; but into ordinary frock an' corduroys he declared he would not get – nor if he had to go naked the rest of his life; so my father, being a good-natured man and handy with the needle, turned to and repaired damages with a piece or two of scarlet cloth cut from the jacket of one of the drowned Marines. Well, the poor little chap chanced to be standing, in this rig-out, down by the gate of Gunner's Meadow, where they had buried two score and over of his comrades. The morning was a fine one, early in March month; and along came the cracked trumpeter, likewise taking a stroll.

' "Hullo!" says he; "good mornin'! And what might you be doin' here?"

' "I was a-wishin'," says the boy, "I had a pair o' drum-sticks. Our lads were buried yonder without so much as a drum tapped or a musket fired; and that's not Christian burial for British soldiers."

' "Phut!" says the trumpeter, and spat on the ground; "a parcel of Marines!"

'The boy eyed him a second or so, and answered up: "If I'd a tab of turf handy, I'd bung it at your mouth, you greasy cavalryman, and learn you to speak respectful of your betters. The Marines are the handiest body of men in the service."

'The trumpeter looked down on him from the height of six foot two, and asked: "Did they die well?"

' "They died very well. There was a lot of running to and fro at first, and some of the men began to cry, and a few to strip off their clothes. But when the ship fell off for the last time, Captain Mein turned and said something to Major Griffiths, the commanding officer on board, and the Major called out to me to beat to quarters. It might have been for a wedding, he sang it out so cheerful. We'd had word already that 'twas to be parade order, and the men fell in as trim and decent as if they were going to church. One or two even tried to shave at the last moment. The Major wore his medals. One of the seamen, seeing I had hard work to keep the drum steady – the sling being a bit loose for me and the wind what you remember – lashed it tight with a piece of rope; and that saved my life afterwards, a drum being as good as a cork until 'tis stove. I kept beating away until every man was on deck; and then the Major formed them up and told them to die like British soldiers, and the chaplain read a prayer or two – the boys standin' all the while like rocks, each man's courage keeping up the others. The chaplain was in the middle of a prayer when she struck. In ten minutes she was gone. That was how they died, cavalryman."

' "And that was very well done, drummer of the Marines. What's your name?"

' "John Christian."

' "Mine is William George Tallifer, trumpeter, of the 7th Light Dragoons – the Queen's Own. I played *God Save the King* while our men were drowning. Captain Duncanfield told me to sound a call or two, to put them in heart; but that matter of *God Save the King* was a notion of my own. I won't say anything to hurt the feelings of a Marine, even if he's not much over five-foot tall; but the Queen's Own Hussars is a tearin' fine regiment. As between horse and foot, 'tis a question o' which gets the chance. All the way from Sahagun to Corunna 'twas we that took and gave the knocks – at Mayorga and Rueda, and Bennyventy." (The reason, sir, I can speak the names so pat is that my father learnt 'em by heart afterwards from the trumpeter, who was always talking about Mayorga and Rueda and Bennyventy.) "We made the rear-guard, under General Paget, and drove the French every time; and all the infantry did was to sit about in wine-shops till we whipped 'em out, an' steal an' straggle an' play the tom-fool in general. And when it came to a stand-up fight at Corunna, 'twas the horse, or the best part of it, that had to stay sea-sick aboard the transports, an' watch the infantry in the thick o' the caper. Very well they behaved, too; 'specially the 4th Regiment, an' the 42nd Highlanders an' the Dirty Half-Hundred. Oh, ay; they're decent regiments, all three. But the Queen's Own Hussars is a tearin' fine regiment. So you played on your drum when the ship was goin' down? Drummer John Christian, I'll have to get you a new pair o' drum-sticks for that."

'Well, sir, it appears that the very next day the trumpeter marched into Helston, and got a carpenter there to turn him a pair of box-wood drumsticks for the boy. And this was the beginning of one of the most curious friendships you ever heard tell of. Nothing delighted the pair more than to borrow a boat off my father and pull out to the rocks where the *Primrose* and the *Despatch* had struck and sunk; and still days 'twas pretty to hear them out there off the Manacles, the drummer playing his tattoo – for they always took their music with them – and the trumpeter practising calls, and making his trumpet speak like an angel. But if the weather turned roughish, they'd be walking together and talking; leastwise, the younger listened while the other discoursed about Sir John's campaign in Spain and Portugal, telling how each little skirmish befell; and of Sir John himself, and General Baird and General Paget, and Colonel Vivian, his own commanding officer, and what kind of men they were; and of the last bloody stand-up at Corunna, and so forth, as if neither could have enough.

'But all this had to come to an end in the late summer; for the boy, John Christian, being now well and strong again, must go up to Plymouth to report himself. 'Twas his own wish (for I believe King George had forgotten all about him), but his friend wouldn't hold him back. As for the trumpeter, my father had made an arrangement to take him on as a lodger as soon as the boy left; and on the morning fixed for the start, he was up at the door here by five o'clock, with his trumpet slung by his side, and all the rest of his kit in a small valise. A Monday morning it was, and after breakfast he had fixed to walk with the boy some way on the road towards Helston, where the coach started. My father left them at breakfast together, and went out to meat the pig, and do a few odd morning jobs of that sort. When he came back, the boy was still at table, and the trumpeter standing here by the chimney-place with the drum and trumpet in his hands, hitched together just as they be at this moment.

' "Look at this," he says to my father, showing him the lock; "I picked it up off a starving brass-worker in Lisbon, and it is not one of your common locks that one word of six letters will open at any time. Ther's *janius* in this lock; for you've only to make the rings spell any six-letter word you please, and snap down the lock upon that, and never a soul can open it – not the maker, even – until somebody comes along that knows the word you snapped it on. Now, Johnny here's goin', and he leaves his drum behind him; for, though he can make pretty music on it, the parchment sags in wet weather, by reason of the sea-water getting at it; an' if he carries it to Plymouth, they'll only condemn it and give him another. And, as for me, I shan't have the heart to put lip to the trumpet any more when Johnny's gone. So we've chosen a word together, and locked 'em together upon that; and, by your leave, I'll hang 'em here together on the hook over your fireplace. Maybe Johnny'll come back; maybe not. Maybe, if he comes, I'll be dead an' gone, an' he'll take 'em apart an' try their music for old sake's sake. But if he never comes, nobody can separate 'em; for nobody beside knows the word. And if you marry and have sons, you can tell 'em that here are tied together the souls of Johnny Christian, drummer of the Marines, and William George Tallifer, once trumpeter of the Queen's Own Hussars. Amen."

'With that he hung the two instruments 'pon the hook there; and the boy stood up and thanked my father and shook hands; and the pair went forth of the door, towards Helston.

'Somewhere on the road they took leave of one another; but nobody saw the parting, nor heard what was said between them. About three in the afternoon the trumpeter came walking back over the hill; and by the time my father came home from the fishing, the cottage was tidied up and the tea ready, and the whole place shining like a new pin. From that time for five years he lodged here with my father, looking after the house and tilling the garden; and all the while he was steadily failing, the hurt in his head spreading, in a manner, to his limbs. My father watched the feebleness growing on him, but said nothing. And from first to last neither spake a word about the drummer, John Christian; nor did any letter reach them, nor word of his doings.

'The rest of the tale you'm free to believe, sir, or not, as you please. It stands upon my father's words, and he always declared he was ready to kiss the Book upon it before judge and jury. He said, too, that he never had the wit to make up such a yarn; and he defied anyone to explain about the lock, in particular, by any other tale. But you shall judge for yourself.

'My father said that about three o'clock in the morning, April fourteenth of the year 'fourteen, he and William Tallifer were sitting here, just as you and I, sir, are sitting now. My father had put on his clothes a few minutes before, and was mending his spiller by the light of the horn lantern, meaning to set off before daylight to haul the trammel. The trumpeter hadn't been to bed at all. Towards the last he mostly spent his nights (and his days, too) dozing in the elbow-chair where you sit at this minute. He was dozing then (my father said), with his chin dropped forward on his chest, when a knock sounded upon the door, and the door opened, and in walked an upright young man in scarlet regimentals.

'He had grown a brave bit, and his face was the colour of wood-ashes; but it was the drummer, John Christian. Only his uniform was different from the one he used to wear, and the figures "38" shone in brass upon his collar.

'The drummer walked past my father as if he never saw him, and stood by the elbow-chair and said:

' "Trumpeter, trumpeter, are you one with me?"

'And the trumpeter just lifted the lids of his eyes, and answered, "How should I not be one with you, drummer Johnny – Johnny boy? The men are patient. 'Till you come, I count; while you march, I mark time; until the discharge comes."

' "The discharge has come tonight," said the drummer, "and the word is Corunna no longer"; and stepping to the chimney-place, he unhooked

c

the drum and trumpet, and began to twist the brass rings of the lock, spelling the word aloud, so – C-O-R-U-N-A. When he had fixed the last letter, the padlock opened in his hand.

' "Did you know, trumpeter, that when I came to Plymouth, they put me into a line regiment?"

' "The 38th is a good regiment," answered the old Hussar, still in his dull voice. "I went back with them from Sahagun to Corunna. At Corunna they stood in General Fraser's division, on the right. They behaved well."

' "But I'd fain see the Marines again," says the drummer, handing him the trumpet; "and you – you shall call once more for the Queen's Own. Matthew," he says, suddenly, turning on my father – and when he turned, my father saw for the first time that his scarlet jacket had a round hole by the breast-bone, and that the blood was welling there – "Matthew, we shall want your boat."

'Then my father rose on his legs like a man in a dream, while they two slung on, the one his drum, and t'other his trumpet. He took the lantern, and went quaking before them down to the shore, and they breathed heavily behind him; and they stepped into his boat, and my father pushed off.

' "Row you first for Dolor Point," says the drummer. So my father rowed them out past the white houses of Coverack to Dolor Point, and there, at a word lay on his oars. And the trumpeter, William Tallifer, put his trumpet to his mouth and sounded the *Revelly*. The music of it was like rivers running.

' "They will follow," said the drummer. "Matthew, pull you now for the Manacles."

'So my father pulled for the Manacles, and came to an easy close outside Carn dû. And the drummer took his sticks and beat a tattoo, there by the edge of the reef; and the music of it was like a rolling chariot.

' "That will do," says he, breaking off; "they will follow. Pull now for the shore under Gunner's Meadow."

'Then my father pulled for the shore, and ran his boat in under Gunner's Meadow. And they stepped out, all three, and walked up to the meadow. By the gate the drummer halted and began his tattoo again, looking out towards the darkness over the sea.

'And while the drum beat, and my father held his breath, there came up out of the sea and the darkness a troop of many men, horse and foot, and formed up among the graves; and others rose out of the graves and formed up – drowned Marines with bleached faces, and pale Hussars riding their horses, all lean and shadowy. There was no clatter of hoofs or accoutrements, my father said, but a soft sound all the while, like the beating of a bird's wing, and a black shadow lying like a pool about the feet of all. The drummer stood upon a little knoll just inside the gate, and beside him the tall trumpeter, with hand on hip, watching them gather; and behind them both my father, clinging to the gate. When no more came, the drummer stopped playing, and said, "Call the roll."

'Then the trumpeter stepped towards the end man of the rank and called, "Troop-Sergeant-Major Thomas Irons!" and the man in a thin voice answered "Here!"

' "Troop-Sergeant-Major Thomas Irons, how is it with you?"

'The man answered, "How should it be with me? When I was young, I betrayed a girl; and when I was grown, I betrayed a friend; and for these things I must pay. But I died as a man ought. God save the King!"

'The trumpeter called to the next man, "Trooper Henry Buckingham!" and the next man answered, "Here!"

' "Trooper Henry Buckingham, how is it with you?"

' "How should it be with me? I was a drunkard, and I stole, and in Lugo, in a wine-shop, I knifed a man. But I died as a man should. God save the King!"

'So the trumpeter went down the line; and when he had finished, the drummer took it up, hailing the dead Marines in their order. Each man answered to his name, and each man ended with "God save the King!" When all were hailed, the drummer stepped back to his mound, and called:

' "It is well. You are content, and we are content to join you. Wait yet a little while."

'With this he turned and ordered my father to pick up the lantern, and lead the way back. As my father picked it up, he heard the ranks of dead men cheer and call "God save the King!" all together, and saw them waver and fade back into the dark, like a breath fading off a pane.

'But when they came back here to the kitchen, and my father set the lantern down, it seemed they'd both forgot about him. For the drummer turned in the lantern-light – and my father could see the blood still welling out of the hole in his breast – and took the trumpet-sling from around the other's neck, and locked drum and trumpet together again, choosing the letters on the lock very carefully. While he did this he said:

' "The word is no more Corunna, but Bayonne. As you left out an 'n' in Corunna, so must I leave out an 'n' in Bayonne." And before snapping the padlock, he spelt out the word slowly – "B-A-Y-O-N-E." After that he used no more speech; but turned and hung the two instruments back on the hook; and then took the trumpeter by the arm; and the pair walked out into the darkness, glancing neither to right nor left.

'My father was on the point of following, when he heard a sort of sigh behind him; and there, sitting in the elbow-chair, was the very trumpeter he had just seen walk out by the door! If my father's heart jumped before, you may believe it jumped quicker now. But after a bit, he went up to the man asleep in the chair, and put a hand upon him. It was the trumpeter in the flesh and blood that he touched; but though the flesh was warm, the trumpeter was dead.

'Well, sir, they buried him three days after; and at first my father was minded to say nothing about his dream (as he thought it). But the day after the funeral, he met Parson Kendall coming from Helston market; and the parson called out: "Have 'ee heard the news the coach brought down this mornin'?" "What news?" says my father. "Why, that peace is agreed upon." "None too soon," says my father. "Not soon enough for our poor lads at Bayonne," the parson answered. "Bayonne!" cries my father, with a jump. "Why, yes"; and the parson told him all about a great sally the French had made on the night of April 13th. "Do you happen to know if the 38th Regiment was engaged?" my father asked. "Come, now," said Parson Kendall, "I didn't know you was so well up in the campaign. But, as it happens, I *do* know that the 38th was engaged, for 'twas they that held a cottage and stopped the French advance."

'Still my father held his tongue; and when, a week later, he walked into Helston and bought a *Mercury* off the Sherborne rider, and got the landlord of the "Angel" to spell out the list of killed and wounded, sure enough, there among the killed was Drummer John Christian, of the 38th Foot.

'After this, there was nothing for a religious man but to make a clean breast. So my father went up to Parson Kendall and told the whole story. The parson listened, and put a question or two, and then asked:

' "Have you tried to open the lock since that night?"

' "I han't dared to touch it," says my father.

' "Then come along and try." When the parson came to the cottage here, he took the things off the hook and tried the lock. "Did he say *'Bayonne'*? The word has seven letters."

' "Not if you spell it with one 'n' as *he* did," says my father.

'The parson spelt it out – B-A-Y-O-N-E. "Whew!" says he, for the lock had fallen open in his hand.

'He stood considering it a moment, and then he says, "I tell you what. I shouldn't blab this all round the parish, if I was you. You won't get no credit for truth-telling, and a miracle's wasted on a set of fools. But if you like, I'll shut down the lock again upon a holy word that no one but me shall know, and neither drummer nor trumpeter, dead nor alive, shall frighten the secret out of me."

' "I wish to gracious you would, parson," said my father.

'The parson chose the holy word there and then, and shut the lock back upon it, and hung the drum and trumpet back in their place. He is gone long since, taking the word with him. And till the lock is broken by force, nobody will ever separate those twain.'

BARBARA SOFTLY

The time of Cromwell and his Roundheads brought into being the first British Army which functioned on the lines clearly recognizable in the present army, but not without birth-pangs. The Defence Cuts of 1647 were aimed at reducing the standing army but did nothing about the soldiers' arrears to pay. At the same time Parliament ruled that, except for General Fairfax, there should be no officers over the rank of colonel. The result was that a sort of Army Trades Union was formed, represented by 'Agitators' – two men from each troop of cavalry.

Things improved over the next ten years but it was wise for the Roundhead in *Master Ghost and I* to make his inheritance secure – even with the aid of such a strange companion.

Barbara Softly (1924–) has published thirteen books since 1961, many of them about the Civil War in which she has a special interest. This story is her only venture into the macabre so far, but it is unlikely to be her last because she is one of the few people who has heard the 'ghostly screaming' associated with Ludlow Castle – a psychical phenomenon yet to be explained.

3 · MASTER GHOST AND I

NATHANIEL DODD, the steward who had served our family for as long as I could remember and who had not seen me for close on five years, stared disapprovingly over the roll of parchment in his hand. His eyes, squinting in the sunlight that dances through the window to make a mockery of the sullen atmosphere, became mere pinpricks that tried to pierce my thoughts. His stare moved from my tanned features to the buff coat of my officer's uniform, travelled down the sleeve and paused on the edge of plain linen at my wrist. Involuntarily, and immediately ashamed of the action, I curved my fingers under my gloves so that he would not notice the nails I had split that morning while mending a broken bridle. From my hands the stare glided to my sword, slid from hilt to tip and came to rest on the spurs of my muddied riding-boots.

'I left as soon as I received your message,' I began in weak apology for my unkempt looks, and feeling momentarily like the refractory schoolboy he still considered me to be.

The squinting eyes swung from my boots to my face again.

'You may sit down,' he said.

Four cold words; not 'Good day' or any remark on the change in my appearance which the half decade of soldiering with the Parliamentary Army must have made. I checked the rising comment, for I had no wish to make a greater enemy of the man who was the sole link with my family who had disowned me.

What had I done? Rebelled. The only one of my parents' four children who had dared to disobey their wishes. My two brothers had, not willingly, directed their lives into the ways chosen for them and my sister, at an early age, had been given in marriage to an elderly landowner of wealth in order to provide him with much-wanted heirs. But I, at fifteen as I then was, had seen little glamour or excitement in the life of a priest when I learned that I was destined for the Church. Glamour, life, excitement were to my mind to be found in my youthful pleasures, my sword, my horse, and the prospect of fighting; but not fighting for King Charles, who had just raised his standard at Nottingham, and who was head of that very Church from which I wished to escape.

A few months after I had run away from home I was tracked down by Nathaniel Dodd. That was the first time I was summoned to receive his disapproving stare and the four cold words – 'You may sit down'. On that occasion I had remained standing, a silent but defiant fifteen-year-old, my hair cropped as short as the most fanatical Roundhead's, determined to retain my freedom. It was not my freedom that Master Dodd wanted. It was to tell me that I could go the way I had chosen and live on the meagre pay of a common soldier because my family had disowned me, and there would never be any forgiveness for me.

'Callous young puppy,' Nathaniel Dodd had hissed at my apparent composure.

'What do you expect me to say?' I had asked, goaded into speech by his contempt. 'If I show sorrow now for the distress I have caused my parents for not entering the Church, you will be the first to tell me my repentance is too late. The Church is not for me. Why should a boy's life be stunted to suit his parents' whim? If they prefer to exile me and make me homeless, they are to blame for their own unhappiness now, not I.'

They were hard words, and they came from a heart that was steeling itself to do without kindred and home for the bitter years of civil war.

Now, five years later, Nathaniel Dodd had sent for me again saying that he had important family matters to divulge. By this time there was a lull in the fighting and I, no longer a common soldier but a captain of a troop of horse in the New Model Army, was able to leave my quarters without a moment's delay. Believing that my father or both my parents were dying, if not dead, I covered the many miles to Master Dodd in two hot summer days, to arrive tired and travel-stained on a well-nigh lamed horse in the mid-afternoon.

'You may sit down.' The words were repeated.

'Thank you,' I replied, and obeyed, flinging my hat and gloves on the floor beside me.

For an instant the pinprick eyes wavered, then dropped to the parchment and began to read. I was conscious that, at the end of every line, Master Dodd's attention wandered from the black script to my relaxed figure, noting my hair, now long like an ordinary officer's, not shorn like a fanatic's, and the air of maturity and experience.

'Are my parents well?' I asked.

He started as if he had not expected me to have the temerity to address him first.

'In exceptional health, I believe,' he said, and there was a hint of acidity in his voice showing that neither I nor what he read on the parchment was to his liking.

'This is your uncle's will,' he continued in the same sour tone. 'Your father's only brother Edward Knapton, who, until within a few months of his death fought loyally at the King's side.' He glared at me over the parchment again and I wondered why he was at pains to tell me this. 'He has left his fortune, which was considerable, not to your father, your brothers or your sister – but – to a rebellious, ill-favoured, traitorous' – and here his list of adjectives failed him – 'ne'er-do-well – to yourself.' He tossed the document in contempt on to the table in front of him.

I hid my amazement at his news and replied with as little sarcasm as possible that my uncle must have known the others were well provided for. If Master Dodd had been a common soldier he would have spat out his disgust.

'The man was mad,' he exploded, 'mad! He destroyed his previous will and made that – that travesty – only a short while ago.' His fingers quivering with fury, he pulled some keys from a drawer and went to a small coffer under the window. 'If you need money now I can let you have some, and the rest can be sent when and where you want it later. The house can be sold and then I –'

'What house?' I interrupted.

'Your uncle's,' he barked. 'Now yours. A new house –' And he named a village deep in a part of the West Country which had been torn by the campaigns during the early years of the war. 'He finished building it this spring and planned to live in it at once, but –' He hesitated, lifting the lid of the chest and burying his hand in its contents. 'It's no place for anyone and you'll not be needing a house when you are on the march all the time – you chose to give up one Royalist home and this will only be another. It will fetch a good price and –'

'I do not wish to sell it,' I replied firmly. His ready acceptance of the fact that I neither needed nor wanted the house roused my obstinate nature, although I was not really inclined to be saddled with the property. 'You can give me the keys and I will go down there.'

He straightened up, his eyes blinking nervously.

'You'll not like it. Your uncle could not abide it in the end.'

'No doubt that was why he left it to me,' I said. 'If he had been fond of it he would have given it to a more worthy recipient. In any case, I should like to see the servants. They might not be willing to serve a rebel master after a Royalist one.'

'There are no servants.' He spoke slowly in order to convey some deeper meaning. 'The place is empty, no one will stay there. Your uncle was driven from it – by some power, some evil – he believed the place was haunted.'

'Haunted?' I laughed. 'What – a house not a year old with a ghost? Who is it? One of the bricklayers fallen from the scaffolding or did they wall up the master carpenter in the chimney because of his prying ways?'

Nathaniel Dodd eyed me with awe and a strange fascination.

'Heaven be praised you never entered the Church,' he muttered. 'The supernatural is to be feared not mocked.'

He passed a bag of money and some keys from the coffer to my outstretched hand. Then smoothed his glistening forehead with a damp palm.

'I shall be ready to sell the property when you have changed your mind,' he said.

I slipped the bag and keys into my pouch, swung my hat and gloves from the floor, and bowed my thanks.

'Maybe I won't change my mind,' I smiled, and I was conscious of the shaft of sunlight dancing joyously across the sombre room. 'For perhaps Master Ghost and I will become well acquainted.'

Forty-eight hours later, on a day that turned from high summer to the cloud and steady wind which had prevailed for most of the season, I sat surveying my inheritance – or what I could see of its chimneys showing above a high, uncut hawthorn hedge and an iron-studded gateway. Dismounting, I glanced all round, back along the grassy track which had led from the road a mile away; to the right where the deep hills were folded in peace, and to the left where from a distant, tree-lined hollow, the smoke from hidden cottage fires was being swept like pennants across the countryside.

I hitched my horse to a stake in the hedge and, leaving him there to graze, fitted one of Master Dodd's keys to the lock on the gate. The key grated, the lock was stiff and the gate had to be pushed over uneven ground where I had thought there would be a smooth drive. There was no drive and I stood staring in bewilderment. There was nothing, nothing but grass, rough and knee-deep or in hummocky tufts and the whole vast hayfield, in which the house and outbuildings seemed to have been dropped, was scattered with mature trees. Only under the nearest line of windows was there a terrace of freshly laid flag-stones, and they were edged with weeds, littered with wisps of straw and flutterings of dead leaves.

What is it that is so uncanny about an empty house? As I moved softly on the carpet of turf every window seemed to be watching, every stone to be listening and the air of desolation was so heavy and still that my ears were oppressed with it. Yet there was no stillness; the silence was full of the wind of that dull, clouded summer day, a wind that swept the dry leaves on the flags, that bent the branches of the limes into brooms and brushed them into never-ending motion; a wind full of unseen voices.

The clattering of my spurs striking the terrace steps was enough to unsteady my nerves; my hand flew to my sword while my heart pounded as it had never done in battle.

'Coward,' I muttered, remembering Master Dodd's words. 'But it seems a day of ghosts; the air could be full of them, crying like lost souls.'

'Will you be wanting anything, sir?'

I spun round, back to the wall, sword half drawn, ready to defend myself against the supernatural if need be.

A most unghostlike face, balanced on the haft of a scythe, was glaring at me through the overgrown bushes.

'I be here to cut the grass,' it said.

'A pity you did not come sooner,' I retorted, angry with myself. 'It has not been cut for months.'

'I come once a year – the Master only wanted me once a year.' The shrubs quivered and a man wriggled on to the stones in front of me. He stood up slowly, stroking the blade of the scythe and eyeing my buff coat with the same look as Master Dodd's – disapproval verging on hatred. 'I'm Mallett,' he said, 'Ned Mallett, and you're a soldier, bain't you.' It was a statement not a question. 'We don't hold with soldiers in these parts; you'd best be off before anyone else sees you.' The scythe tilted in the manner of a battle-axe.

'This is my house,' I told him. 'The master of whom you speak was my uncle and he has left this property to me.'

'That's as maybe,' he growled. 'Master or no master, you're a soldier, and we've had enough of soldiery in these parts whether they be King's men or Parliament's. You leave peaceful folks be.'

'The previous owner, Edward Knapton, was a soldier, too,' I replied.

'Maybe he was.' The man's attitude became more threatening. 'But we don't want no more of you, trampling our crops, eating our food, burning our barns, taking all, and paying nothing. We fought you once with pitchforks and clubs and we'll fight you again whether you be the Master, the King, or the Parliament.'

I knew what he meant. Villagers all over that locality, driven to desperation by the plunder of war, had banded together to fight the common enemy, Royalist and Roundhead. Both sides had tried to woo their friendship with promises of better-disciplined troops and gifts of muskets and carbines. The Clubmen, we had called them, because of their primitive weapons.

'You'd better be going,' he said again before I could speak. 'Master Knapton wouldn't stay here. Worried wellnigh out of his wits, he was, though it wasn't us what drove him away. It might have been,' he added menacingly, 'if the devil hadn't done it for us. "I'll not come again," that's what he told me. "Ned Mallett," he said, "the place is evil and I'll not –" '

'Never mind what he told you,' I interrupted, my temper rising. 'You and your Clubmen, the devil and all his demons, I am staying here the night at least. So you "had best be off" down to those cottages and find someone who can come up and cook supper for me. My horse needs stabling, too, and you can do that on your way back.'

He wavered under the decisive tones, but, as his eyes shifted over my shoulder, something more like cunning crept into his voice.

'My missus'll come up like she did for Master Edward,' he muttered. 'She'll do the fires and air the linen – though she'll not –'

'I am not asking anyone to sleep here,' I forestalled him, and immediately thought that I should feel safer in my bed with my hostile neighbours on the other side of a barred door. 'I am not afraid of being alone.'

Without another word, he jerked the scythe into his hands and went towards the outbuildings on a path that was evidently the shortest route to the cottages in the hollow. I moved to recross the terrace to the main porch, intending to explore the house, for I was anxious to examine it thoroughly before the man and his wife returned or darkness fell.

With an exclamation of annoyance, I saw another prying villager standing behind me, a boy of about fifteen years of age.

'Who are you?' I snapped.

'Ro-Roger,' he stammered.

'And you live here, too, I suppose?'

'S-Sort of.'

We looked each other up and down.

'You – you're a soldier,' he said. 'A soldier in the New Model Army, an officer.'

'A captain of a troop of horse, and before that I served under Waller in most of his campaigns here in the West; and I have been a soldier for the past five years.'

I rolled the words out in fury, waiting for the inevitable disapproval, but it did not come. The boy was staring at me with an odd mixture of incredulity, wonderment, and admiration. His hair was cropped shorter than mine had ever been and he was wearing a shabby doublet and breeches of a faded blue-grey colour. On second thoughts, as I continued to study him, I decided that his clothes were not shabby with the wear of work as Ned Mallett's had been. They were faded with disuse, the lace of his shirt yellowed, dust in the creases of folding, and it seemed probable that he was dressed in a discarded suit of my uncle's.

'You knew Master Knapton?' I asked. 'Master Edward Knapton who lived here?'

'He only came once, a short while ago. I met him then,' was the quick reply.

'And he gave you those clothes?'

A momentary glimmer of astonishment showed in the boy's eyes and he glanced down at his doublet.

'They came from the chest at the foot of his bed,' he explained, and then more eagerly, 'Why are you here? You're a soldier, and there's no fighting now.'

'Because the house is mine.' Soon these villagers will be aware of that fact, I thought. 'Edward Knapton was my uncle, and I am John Knapton, his nephew, who –'

'John Knapton?' he broke in. 'You are John Knapton? But – but you're a soldier – a captain in the Army –' His astonishment was not hidden now. 'But no one would ever have dreamed you were a Roundhead soldier as well.'

'As well as what?' I asked.

He flushed, hesitated, and shrugged his shoulders.

'As well as – being – being –'

'As well as being the nephew of a loyal subject of the King,' I finished for him.

He smiled and the flush deepened.

'That's as good a reason as any.'

He laughed, and I could not help liking the boy; his disarming friendliness and his quaint, clipped way of speaking, which was quite different from Mallett's broad dialect or my slight country drawl.

Taking out another of Master Dodd's keys, I went towards the door at the front of the house, and as I reached the porch I heard Roger padding softly after me.

'This is tansy, isn't it?' he asked.

I turned and saw him running his hand up a feathery-leaved yellow flower which was growing in a straggling clump at the edge of the steps. He buried his nose in his palm.

'What a scent!' he exclaimed. 'It reminds me of blazing borders and summer gardens.'

'It reminds me of fleas,' I said, 'and doses of bitter physic when I was a child.'

His guffaw of laughter warmed me. It was good to hear such a sound in the atmosphere of cheerlessness which had so far been my greeting. When I opened the door, wrinkling my nose at the musty smell, Roger was close at my elbow.

He wriggled past my arm. 'Look,' he whispered in excitement. 'It's new – so new. Look at the panelling and this floor.' He darted across the hall to smooth his fingers down the freshly carved woodwork on the walls.

'Of course it's new, boy,' I replied. 'It was only finished this year. Didn't you see it when my uncle was here?'

He shook his head. 'I – I didn't come in,' he murmured, and with an effort seemed to check his eagerness.

After that, with firmly compressed lips, he followed me like a dog, through the living-rooms and kitchens, stopping when I stopped, and pausing to look out of a window whenever I opened one. Upstairs, in one of the bedrooms which was more fully furnished than the rest of the house and had obviously been intended for my uncle's use, the sour staleness was overpowering. As I strode to the window, out of the corner of my eye, I saw Roger drop on his knees in front of the linen chest at the foot of the four-poster bed. With a sigh of pleasure, he let his fingers caress the dull wood as they had caressed the panelling and the yellow herb.

'It's the same,' I heard him hiss. 'It's unbelievable that it's still the same only so much darker.'

'If it's the one Master Knapton took your suit from I'm not surprised it's the same,' I said, glancing round at him. 'But as you did not come indoors when he was here, I don't see how you can recognize it.'

He dropped back on his heels as if caught in some guilty thought of action.

'The date is on it here,' I said quietly, for he did not reply, and I seemed to have damped his enthusiasm. 'On the lid – 1620. I've no doubt it was made for my uncle when he was a young man. It's old by his standards now, over twenty-five years.'

'Twenty-five years! That's not old,' Roger protested. 'It won't look like that in over three hundred years, that I know.'

'Neither will you,' I retorted.

He stared at me. There was silence, a second's silence while the wind of that dull, clouded summer day blew in the narrow window and sent only its voices sweeping through my uncle's room.

' *"Tempus edax rerum",'* I commented.

'What?' asked Roger sharply. 'What does that mean? It's Latin, isn't it?'

'Latin, boy!' I exclaimed. 'Of course it's Latin, and at your age you should know what it means.'

'I don't,' he confessed. 'I don't take Latin at my school. I take other subjects.'

I refrained from another exclamation. For all I knew he might be some ignorant local lad that my uncle had befriended and he was trying to cover his lack of knowledge by blaming it on to his schoolmaster.

' "Time, the devourer of all things," is a fair enough translation,' I explained.

Roger's eyes met mine, and again I was conscious of the wind, the rustle of the dead lime flowers on the flags. Then he chuckled – and the sound of hoofs clopping on the terrace beneath us told me that Ned Mallett had returned to stable my horse. I hurried to the head of the stairs to see if the man's wife was with him too. Before I called down I glanced back at Roger. He had not moved but he was watching me, that strange look of wonder, near affection, on his face. Although I pretended not to have noticed, it was with growing feelings of uneasiness and foreboding that I made my way to the kitchen.

Who was he, this boy? He seemed familiar with my uncle's possessions, and yet he said he had only met him once. Was his friendliness genuine or was it a cloak for something deeper? Ned Mallett's antagonism had unsettled me. I recollected his hasty glance to where the boy must have been standing behind me and I began to wonder if, ever since Edward Knapton's death, the villagers had set a spy to wait for the new unwanted soldier-owner of the property; a spy who would gain his confidence, as this boy was gaining mine, and then, at the chosen moment – my fingers sought the hilt of my sword. With that alone, for I now realized my foolishness in leaving my pistols on my saddle, I reckoned I could withstand any treachery.

In the kitchen Mistress Mallett had already lighted the fire and blown it into a blaze. There were clean sheets, which she told me she had brought herself, draped across a bench; but her sullen greeting added to the wave of depression that had come over me at the top of the stairs.

Strong hands smoothed the folds of her petticoats down her broad hips as she regarded me with the eyes of Nathaniel Dodd and Ned Mallett.

'So – you're a soldier,' she sniffed. 'We've seen more than enough of the likes of you.'

'So I understand,' was my quick rejoinder and, leaving her at the oven, I went into the living-room.

'There's bread and cheese and ale for your supper,' she called out. 'I'll make up the beds and then you must shift for yourself. I'll not stay after dusk in this God-forsaken place.'

I did not trouble to reply, but dropped my hat and gloves on the settle as I passed and dragged a high-backed chair up to the table in the window. Sitting there, gazing out over the windswept terrace and the unending grass of that vast field, my depression deepened. Master Dodd had been right; I should have to sell 'the God-forsaken place'. The villagers, even if they intended me no real harm, would never accept me without a

D

struggle, and no doubt, one night spent alone in the house would be enough to drive me away. It would not be difficult to decide which had the most power, the supernatural or the ill-wishes of Master Mallett.

And what of Roger? Was I to be completely alone? It was unlikely after Mistress Mallett's use of the word 'beds'. As far as I could see the boy had no intentions of leaving me, which seemed further confirmation of my suspicions. He had followed me to the kitchen, through to the living-room and now, without turning my head, I was able to watch his form, grey-blue in the growing shadows, where he was crouching on the settle. My hat and gloves were in his lap and he was engrossed, examining both in minute detail – furtively fingering the felt, the leather, even the lines of stitching.

'It's getting dark in here,' I said abruptly.

He started in alarm.

'D-dark?' he stammered. 'I'll switch the light on.'

He sprang across the room to the door and put his hand to the wall. Then he stood still, his hand slipping to his side.

'What's the matter?' I asked, shaken by his words and attitude.

'Candles – I'll fetch the candles,' he murmured.

I stood up to follow him, but hesitated at the strident tones of Mistress Mallett's voice.

'There's candles and tinder in the dresser in the living-room, I'll be bound. Don't you be bothering me, now. The supper's out here and I'll be gone in less than a minute.'

Roger returned. He walked past the dresser, straight to the table, and sat down.

'She doesn't want me in the kitchen at the moment,' he explained. 'There are plenty of candles out there and I'll light them from the fire when she has gone.'

It was a barefaced lie.

'One candle will be sufficient,' I remarked coldly, and sat down opposite.

'I don't mind being in the dark,' he said.

No, I thought in agreement, I do not suppose you do. So much can be accomplished in the dark with an unwary opponent, but I am as watchful as you, my lad.

Suddenly he leaned across and looked searchingly up into my face.

'You know what you said just now, about time,' he began. ' "Time the devourer of all things" – *"tempus"*, something or other?'

' *"Tempus edax rerum"*,' I repeated, wedging my knee under the table so that it could not be tipped unexpectedly and send me off my balance.

'Do you believe that?'

'That time devours everything?' I asked, and I heard the click of the latch as Mistress Mallett left the kitchen. 'It is obvious it does. Look at the grass out there and the hedge. A few months and the place is a wilderness, a few years more of neglect and the whole house will be a tangle of briars, the woodwork rotten and the plaster fallen in. That's time; time devours and –'

'I know,' he interrupted impatiently. 'That's one sort of time – but I'm trying to talk about something else – a – a time that is only a cover, that we have to live by in hours and days, but which doesn't really exist.'

If you are spinning out the time, I thought, you are going about it in a very odd way.

'I'm so hopeless at expressing myself,' he went on with a hint of desperation. 'Something like it comes in a piece of poetry, though I'm not much good at the stuff and I can never remember it properly –

> *"In every land thy feet may tread*
> *Time like a veil is round thy head.*
> *Only the land thou seek'st with me*
> *Never hath been nor yet shall be –"* '

An uneasy cold crept over my whole body as I listened, held against my will by his glowing eyes and the tense face so white in the half light. If he had wanted to put me off my guard, he had succeeded.

'Don't you believe that time is only a veil and if you lift it, you can be anywhere at any period of existence?' he whispered.

Uncertainty, vague fear, and a presentiment of some unknown power gripped me.

' *"Time like a veil is round thy head."* ' The slow words he repeated dropped into the hollow stillness of the empty house.

My question hovered on the air.

'Who wrote that?' I breathed.

'Henry Newbolt,' he said, and even before he spoke I sensed it would be a poet of whom I had never heard.

A sudden flicker of light beyond the hedge in the darkening garden jerked me from my stupor. One hand flew to my sword, the other instinctively closed over Roger's slim wrists on the table. 'Don't move,' I hissed as I pressed him to the chair.

'I can't,' he growled. 'And there's no need to hold me down. I'm not frightened of them.'

The injured tone was reassuring. The boy was no accomplice, of that I was sure, though what he was I had not the courage to admit. I was only concerned at that moment with the need for speedy action.

'I'll wager it's Ned Mallett with his scythe and half the village too, come to drive the soldier from his strong-hold,' I muttered in rising anger. 'And this soldier will not be driven. I'll go of my own free will, and neither man nor devil shall frighten me out of my own house.'

I released Roger who was writhing under the strength of my arm.

'Get down to that gate opposite the terrace steps. See that it's locked and bolted,' I commanded. 'They'll not venture over this hawthorn hedge without ladders yet.'

'Can't we barricade the house?' he asked eagerly. 'We could block all the doors and shutter the windows and pour buckets of blazing tar on their heads. That's what they do in sieges.'

'This isn't a siege,' I snapped, ignoring his flippancy although he appeared to be in earnest. 'And it is not going to be one. Attack first, defence afterwards is the order in my troop of horse. There must be another gate behind the stables and I'll wait for you there.'

He darted away and sent the chair flying in his impetuous dash.

'Don't be foolhardy,' I called. 'If they are armed they'll fire.'

'What?' he paused in the doorway. 'With one of those old carbines? Those things wouldn't hit a cow at five yards.'

'They've been known to kill a man at twenty,' I retorted.

'Oh for a Winchester, and I'd pick 'em off like flies,' he cried.

'I want no bloodshed,' I ordered. Again this remark was incomprehensible, but time enough to ask him what he meant later, I thought. 'If they want to live in peace, far be it from me to start a fight, but they must learn to leave me in peace, too.'

If I could retrieve my pistols – if Master Mallett had not had the wits to remove them from the holsters in anticipation of this attack – and could fire over their heads to frighten them into parleying, we might be able to come to amicable terms after all.

As the outer door banged behind Roger, I groped through the dim kitchen to make my way to the stables and barns – but I never reached either. The moment my foot stepped into the sullen darkness of the clouded evening, a bullet shattered the window at my side. I ducked, slid beneath the covering bushes, and flattened myself against the wall waiting for the next shot. None came; no sound, no movement but the trees in the wind and my own shallow breathing. So much for the prospects of peace without bloodshed, I thought, and this was a form of fighting I despised. With my pistols or sword, even my bare hands, I would tackle any numbers if they refused to listen to words of reason, but this game of hide-and-seek, with an enemy who had already spotted me, was not to my liking.

Cautiously I edged sideways, aware that my disadvantage lay in the fact that I was not familiar with the courtyard, and that the stables might be any of the shapes that rose up in the gloom. If my enemy meant to kill, once I was in the open I was an easy target, and so until I could catch a glimpse of him, it was wiser to hug the wall. My fingers, spreading along the bricks, touched first climbing tendrils, a snail – then, something warm and rough – a hand! I froze. My fingers crept upwards to touch a sleeve. With an exclamation of alarm the owner of the sleeve jerked backwards, and before another hand could drop on mine I sprang at the hidden figure. Nose to nose, knee to knee, we struggled under the bushes betraying our whereabouts to the unseen marksman. His second shot speeding through the branches over my head so startled my antagonist that, in his momentary hesitation, I wrenched myself free, swung my fist and gave him a crushing blow on the jaw. As his sagging body toppled another shape leapt for my throat, received the toe of my jackboot in his stomach and fell winded and writhing to the ground.

Two, I thought quickly, and how many more? Off balance and reeling from my shelter I nearly slipped beneath the double onslaught of a burly figure in front and little, leech-like arms which clasped my wrists behind me. With a vicious kick to the rear, I felt my spurs gouge deeply into a stockinged shin – there was a scream of pain and the third assailant dropped from the fight. But the fourth was taking all my strength; he tripped my feet and sent me sprawling to the dust, bruised and entangled by my own sword, and there we rolled, locked in each other's arms until I became conscious of a light wavering towards us from the darkness of the hedge. It was Master Mallett, a flaming torch held high, and at his side was the marksman with his carbine.

'This is your doing,' I bellowed in a brief moment when I was uppermost. 'I came in peace and if any of these men are dead, may it lie on your conscience for ever.'

I saw the light glinting along the raised barrel and I saw Roger leaping into the circle of yellow flame.

'Get down – he'll fire!' I gasped.

For a moment he stood there poised, a pace from the carbine's mouth – a shot – silence – a feather of smoke – a quiver from the torch as Ned Mallett turned, too late, and struck the gun from the man's hands. The fellow gripping my shoulders loosed them, sat back and eased his bruised muscles; other shapes rose and shambled towards the gate. I lurched to my feet and stumbled forward.

Roger had not moved; upright and as firm as a rock, he watched me coming, a faint smile on his lips. His eyes, as he glanced up into my face, wore an odd, distant look.

'That must be like the silver bullet in the fairy stories that's supposed to kill the devil,' he said quietly. 'It doesn't really kill him, it just gets rid of him for a while.'

'You're hurt,' I said.

I slipped my arm round his shoulders and he did not resist. Slowly I led him to the long grass at the edge of the terrace, where I pulled off my coat and spread it on the ground. He sank down and let his head droop on to the improvised pillow. Kneeling by his side I fumbled with the worn cloth of his doublet, feeling through his shirt to his chest. There was not a mark on him nor a speck of blood.

'There's no wound,' I whispered.

'There won't be,' he murmured. 'I'm not going to die yet. I shall be alive long after you are dead – more than three hundred years.'

I gazed into that still face which glimmered among the grasses like a white moth at rest.

He raised one hand; his fingers touched my hair, my cheek, my linen shirt, the hilt of my unused sword.

'John Knapton – Captain John Knapton,' and I sensed that he was smiling. 'I have always wanted to know what you were really like – and now I know you were a Roundhead soldier as well, while everyone else just believes you to be the man who laid out the gardens.'

'What gardens?' I asked, a great fear gripping me.

'The gardens here,' he replied. 'Gardens that everyone comes to see – the sundial on the terrace where you carved your name and put those strange words along its rim, in English, too. I wonder why you did that; most people of your time would have put them in Latin. It's so short, so short a time,' he whispered desperately. 'There was so much I wanted to see, to know, to ask – and I never guessed how it could end – I – thought I could be here for ever, if I wanted. The suit was in the chest; I found it there, all folded and old, just as he had put it away and then I hoped I might meet you.' He chuckled. 'I frightened him, the old man, your uncle, though the villagers thought I was some boy of his. It was too soon and I pestered the life out of him asking what he was doing in your house – everyone knew it was yours – they hadn't a clue it belonged to him first – they even thought you built it.'

His fingers slipped from my sword and lay, a feather-weight on my own.

'He was afraid of me,' he murmured. 'I was something out of this world to him, I suppose.'

I heard the wind bending the lime branches, the leaves tapping the flagstones, but there were no voices, only peace in that clouded night.

'The supernatural is to be feared not mocked,' Master Dodd had said – and I was not afraid.

I watched him, how long I watched him, I cannot tell. His slight form lay, a shadow in the flattened grass, his face fading, until, as the moonless hours crept by, he drifted like a moth into the darkness.

My coat was warm when I took it up and stumbled into the house. I lit a candle with the tinder that I believed Roger had not known how to use and mounted the stairs to my uncle's room. There I opened the chest and there I found the blue-grey doublet and breeches, the fine lace shirt, fresh-folded in lavender, just as my uncle had laid them away a few months ago; the dust and creases, the yellowing of age and faded colours that Roger had put on would form with the years, three hundred years of time.

I knelt there, my head bowed in my arms while the candle burned low in its socket. I, who had never allowed myself to feel the need for a home, now wanted this, my inheritance, though willed to me in fear; and wanted to create out of its wilderness something living to take the place of the destruction which had been five years of my life.

Was it possible, I asked myself, to raise a memorial to a ghost from the future, to a boy not yet born, a memorial that would endure until he came?

'A wall would not last longer than that hawthorn hedge,' I thought. 'And oaks are slower growing than limes or elms; flagged paths and stone seats would weather the centuries; shrubs of rosemary and lavender – they spring from slips quick enough although the mother plant may not thrive more than a decade and' – I laughed aloud – 'he shall have his tansy and as many herbs as he wants, descendants of the ones already here; and his blazing borders, banked by yew – that's almost everlasting.'

I stubbed the flaring candle in its pool of grease and, fired with enthusiasm, strode to the open window. The limes were still, only an early thrush was rustling the limp leaves.

'A dial on the terrace,' I mused, 'where it will catch the sun most of the day; and my name on it with some Latin maxim carved along its rim, *Tempus Fugit* or –' A chuckle of merriment burst from me. 'But the boy doesn't know any Latin!' I exclaimed. 'Roger, Roger, what an ignorant lad you are – but for your sake, I'll put the words in English.'

I gazed out across the vast field of rampant grass, already seeing in my mind the beauty it was to become. And Roger? I should look for him in vain, for he would not come in my lifetime any more; but come, at last, he would, and love that garden as I was beginning to love it.

' "Long looked for – come at last." ' I breathed into that first dawn the words which were to be inscribed in stone.

The sun's gold touched the latticed panes.

'I have lived three centuries in half a day,' I thought, and then a mischievous smile curved my lips because I knew I should have to write to Nathaniel Dodd.

The house would not be sold for – Master Ghost and I had become well acquainted.

JOHN GALT

John Galt (1779–1839) was a Scottish novelist and an adventurer and pioneer in the old Scottish tradition. He emigrated to Canada where he opened up a road between Lakes Erie and Huron in 1826 and became so celebrated that the town of Galt, Ontario, was named after him.

Returning to his native Irvine, he settled down to writing but was known to protest 'What a cursed fellow that Walter Scott has been to drive me out of my original line'.

The Black Ferry excels any work of Scott's for dour atmosphere and inevitable doom. It is set in the time when Britain was creating an Empire in the East and many a Scot found advancement in the armed forces – but advancement is not everything.

4 · THE BLACK FERRY

I was then returning from my first session at college. The weather had for some time been uncommonly wet, every brook and stream was swollen far beyond its banks, the meadows were flooded, and the river itself was increased to a raging Hellespont, insomuch that the ferry was only practicable for an hour before and after high tide.

The day was showery and stormy, by which I was detained at the inn until late in the afternoon, so that it was dark before I reached the house, and the tide did not serve for safe crossing until midnight. I was therefore obliged to sit by the fire and wait the time, a circumstance which gave me some uneasiness, for the ferryman was old and infirm, and Dick his son, who usually attended the boat during the night, happened to be then absent, the day having been such that it was not expected any travellers would seek to pass over that night.

The presence of Dick was not, however, absolutely necessary, for the boat swung from side to side by a rope anchored in the middle of the stream, and, on account of the strong current, another rope had been stretched across by which passengers could draw themselves over without assistance, an easy task to those who had the sleight of it, but it was not so to me, who still wore my arm in a sling.

While sitting at the fireside conversing with the ferryman and his wife, a smart, good-looking country lad, with a recruit's cockade in his hat, came in, accompanied by a young woman who was far advanced in pregnancy. They were told the state of the ferry, and that unless the recruit undertook to conduct the boat himself, they must wait the return of Dick.

They had been only that day married, and were on their way to join a detachment of the regiment in which Ralph Nocton, as the recruit was called, had that evening enlisted, the parish officers having obliged him to marry the girl. Whatever might have been their former love and intimacy, they were not many minutes in the house when he became sullen and morose towards her; nor was she more amiable towards him. He said little, but he often looked at her with an indignant eye, as she reproached him for having so rashly enlisted, to abandon her and his unborn baby, assuring him that she would never part from him while life and power lasted.

Though it could not be denied that she possessed both beauty and an attractive person, there was yet a silly vixen humour about her ill calculated to conciliate. I did not therefore wonder to hear that Nocton had married her with reluctance; I only regretted that the parish officers were so inaccessible to commiseration, and so void of conscience as to be guilty of rendering the poor fellow miserable for life to avert the hazard of the child becoming a burden on the parish.

The ferryman and his wife endeavoured to reconcile them to their lot; and the recruit, who appeared to be naturally reckless and generous, seemed willing to be appeased; but his weak companion was capricious and pettish. On one occasion, when a sudden shower beat hard against the window, she cried out, with little regard to decorum, that she would go no farther that night.

'You may do as you please, Mary Blake,' said Nocton, 'but go I must, for the detachment marches tomorrow morning. It was only to give you time to prepare to come with me that the Captain consented to let me remain so late in the town.'

She, however, only remonstrated bitterly at his cruelty in forcing her to travel, in her condition, and in such weather. Nocton refused to listen to her, but told her somewhat doggedly, more so than was consistent with the habitual cheerful cast of his physiognomy, 'that although he had already been ruined by her, he trusted she had not yet the power to make him a deserter'.

He then went out, and remained some time alone. When he returned, his appearance was surprisingly changed; his face was of an ashy paleness; his eyes bright, febrile and eager, and his lip quivered as he said:

'Come, Mary, I can wait no longer; the boat is ready, the river is not so wild, and the rain is over.'

In vain she protested; he was firm; and she had no option but either to go or to be left behind. The old ferryman accompanied them to the boat, saw them embark, and gave the recruit some instruction how to manage the ropes, as it was still rather early in the tide. On returning into the house, he remarked facetiously to his wife:

'I can never see why young men should be always blamed, and all pity reserved for the damsels.'

At this moment a rattling shower of rain and hail burst like a platoon of small shot on the window, and a flash of vivid lightning was followed by one of the most tremendous peals of thunder I have ever heard.

'Hark!' cried the old woman, starting, 'was not that a shriek?' We listened, but the cry was not repeated; we rushed to the door, but no other sound was heard than the raging of the river, and the roar of the sea-waves breaking on the bar.

Dick soon after came home, and the boat having swung back to her station, I embarked with him, and reached the opposite inn, where I soon went to bed. Scarcely had I laid my head on the pillow when a sudden inexplicable terror fell upon me; I shook with an unknown horror; I was, as it were, conscious that some invisible being was hovering beside me, and could hardly muster fortitude enough to refrain from rousing the house. At last I fell asleep; it was perturbed and unsound; strange dreams and vague fears scared me awake, and in them were dreadful images of a soldier murdering a female, and open graves, and gibbet-irons swinging in the wind. My remembrance has no parallel to such another night.

In the morning the cloud on my spirit was gone, and I rose at my accustomed hour, and cheerily resumed my journey. It was a bright morning, all things were glittering and fresh in the rising sun, the recruit and his damsel were entirely forgotten, and I thought no more of them.

But when the night returned next year I was seized with an unaccountable dejection; it weighed me down; I tried to shake it off, but was unable; the mind was diseased, and could no more by resolution shake off its discomfort, than the body by activity can expel a fever. I retired to my bed greatly depressed, but nevertheless I fell asleep. At midnight, however, I was summoned to awake by a hideous and undefinable terror; it was the same vague consciousness of some invisible visitor being near that I had once before experienced, as I have described, and I again recollected Nocton and Mary Blake in the same instant; I saw – for I cannot now believe that it was less than apparitional – the unhappy pair reproaching one another.

As I looked, questioning the integrity of my sight, the wretched bride turned round and looked at me. How shall I express my horror, when, for the ruddy beauty which she once possessed, I beheld the charnel visage of a skull? I started up and cried aloud with such alarming vehemence that the whole inmates of the house, with lights in their hands, were instantly in the room – shame would not let me tell what I had seen, and, endeavouring to laugh, I accused the nightmare of the disturbance.

This happened while I was at a watering-place on the west coast. I was living in a boarding-house with several strangers; among them was a tall pale German gentleman, of a grave impressive physiognomy. He was the most intelligent and shrewdest observer I have ever met with, and he had to a singular degree the gift of a discerning spirit. In the morning when we rose from the breakfast-table, he took me by the arm, and led me out upon the lawn in front of the house; and when we were at some distance from the rest of the company, said:

'Excuse me, sir, for I must ask an impertinent question. Was it indeed the dream of the nightmare that alarmed you last night?'

'I have no objection to answer you freely; but tell me first why you ask such a question?'

'It is but reasonable. I had a friend who was a painter; none ever possessed an imagination which discerned better how nature in her mysteries should appear. One of his pictures was the scene of Brutus when his evil genius summoned him to Philippi, and strange to tell, you bear some resemblance to the painted Brutus. When, with the others, I broke into your room last night, you looked so like the Brutus in his picture that I could have sworn you were amazed with the vision of a ghost.'

I related to him what I have done to you.

'It is wonderful,' said he, 'what inconceivable sympathy hath linked you to the fate of these unhappy persons. There is something more in this renewed visitation than the phantasma of a dream.'

The remark smote me with an uncomfortable sensation of dread, and for a short time my flesh crawled as it were upon my bones. But the impression soon wore off, and was again entirely forgotten.

When the anniversary again returned, I was seized with the same heaviness and objectless horror of mind; it hung upon me with bodings and auguries until I went to bed, and then after my first sleep I was a third time roused by another fit of the same inscrutable panic. On this occasion, however, the vision was different. I beheld only Nocton, pale and wounded, stretched on a bed, and on the coverlet lay a pair of new epaulettes, as if just unfolded from a paper.

For seven years I was thus annually afflicted. The vision in each was different, but I saw no more of Mary Blake. On the fourth occasion, I

beheld Nocton sitting in the uniform of an aide-de-camp at a table, with
the customary tokens of conviviality before him; it was only part of a
scene, such as one beholds in a mirror.

On the fifth occasion, he appeared to be ascending, sword in hand, the
rampart of a battery; the sun was setting behind him, and the shadows and
forms of a strange land, with the domes and pagodas of an oriental
country, lay in wide extent around; it was a picture, but far more vivid than
painting can exhibit.

On the sixth time, he appeared again stretched upon a couch; his
complexion was sullen, not from wounds, but disease, and there appeared
at his bedside the figure of a general officer, with a star on his breast, with
whose conversation he appeared pleased, though languid.

But on the seventh and last occasion on which the horror of the visions
were repeated, I saw him on horseback in a field of battle; and while I
looked at him, he was struck on the face by a sabre, and the blood flowed
down upon his regimentals.

Years passed after this, during which I had none of these dismal
exhibitions. My mind and memory resumed their healthful tone. I recollected, without these intervening years of oblivion, Nocton and Mary
Blake occasionally, as one thinks past, and I told my friends of the curious
periodical returns of the visitations to me as remarkable metaphysical
phenomena. By an odd coincidence, it so happened that my German friend
was always present when I related my dreams. He in the intervals spoke to
me of them, but my answers were vague, for my reminiscences were
imperfect. It was not so with him. All I told he distinctly recorded and
preserved in a book wherein he wrote down the minutest thing that I had
witnessed in my visions. I do not mention his name, because he is a modest
and retiring man, in bad health, and who has long sequestered himself from
company. His rank, however, is so distinguished that his name could not
be stated without the hazard of exposing him to impertinent curiosity. But
to proceed.

Exactly fourteen years – twice seven it was – I remember well, because
for the first seven I had been haunted as I have described, and for the other
seven I had been placid in my living. At the end of that period of fourteen
years, my German friend paid me a visit here. He came in the forenoon,
and we spent an agreeable day together, for he was a man of much
recondite knowledge. I have seen none so wonderfully possessed of all

sorts of occult learning.

He was an astrologer of true kind, for on him it was not a pretence but a science; he scorned horoscopes and fortune-tellers with the just derision of a philosopher, but he had a beautiful conception of the reciprocal dependencies of nature. He affected not to penetrate to causes, but he spoke of effects with a luminous and religious eloquence. He described to me how the tides followed the phases of the moon; but he denied the Newtonian notion that they were caused by the procession of the lunar changes. He explained to me that when the sun entered Aries, and the other signs of the zodiac, how his progression could be traced on this earth by the development of plants and flowers, and the passions, diseases, and affections of animals and men; but that the stars were more than the celestial signs of these terrestrial phenomena he ridiculed as the conceptions of the insane theory.

His learning in the curious art of alchemy was equally sublime. He laughed at the fancy of an immortal elixir, and his notion of the mythology of the philosopher's stone was the very essence and spirituality of ethics. The elixir of immortality he described to me as an allegory, which, from its component parts, emblems of talents and virtues, only showed that perseverance, industry, goodwill, and a gift from God were the requisite ingredients necessary to attain renown.

His knowledge of the philosopher's stone was still more beautiful. He referred to the writings of the Rosicrucians, whose secrets were couched in artificial symbols, to prove that the sages of that sect were not the fools that the lesser wise of later days would represent them. The self-denial, the patience, the humility, the trusting in God, the treasuring of time by lamp and calculation which the venerable alchemists recommended, he used to say, were only the elements which constitute the conduct of the youth that would attain to riches and honour; and these different stages which are illuminated in the alchemical volumes as descriptive of stages in the process of making the stone were but hieroglyphical devices to explain the effects of well-applied human virtue and industry.

To me it was amazing to what clear simplicity he reduced all things, and on what a variety of subjects his bright and splendid fancy threw a fair and effecting light. All those demi-sciences – physiognomy, palmistry, scaileology, etc., even magic and witchcraft, obtained from his interpretations a philosophical credibility.

E

In disquisitions on these subjects we spent the anniversary. He had by them enlarged the periphery of my comprehension; he had added to my knowledge, and inspired me with a profounder respect for himself.

He was an accomplished musician, in the remotest, if I may use the expression, depths of the art. His performance on the pianoforte was simple, heavy, and seemingly the labour of an unpractised hand, but his expression was beyond all epithet exquisite and solemn; his airs were grave, devotional, and pathetic, consisting of the simplest harmonic combinations; but they were wonderful; every note was a portion of an invocation; every melody the voice of a passion or a feeling supplied with elocution.

We had spent the days in the fields, where he illustrated his astrological opinions by appeals to plants, and leaves, and flowers, and other attributes of the season, with such delightful perspicuity that no time can efface from the registers of my memory the substance of his courses. In the evening he delighted me with his miraculous music, and, as the night advanced, I was almost persuaded that he was one of those extraordinary men who are said sometimes to acquire communion with spirits and dominion over demons.

Just as we were about to sit down to our frugal supper, literally or philosophically so, as if it had been served for Zeno himself, Dick, the son of the old ferryman, who by this time was some years dead, came to the door, and requested to speak with me in private. Of course I obeyed, when he informed me that he had brought across the ferry that night a gentleman officer, from a far country, who was in bad health, and whom he could not accommodate properly in the ferry-house.

'The inn,' said Dick, 'is too far off, for he is lame, and has an open wound in the thigh. I have therefore ventured to bring him here, sure that you will be glad to give him a bed for the night. His servant tells me that he was esteemed the bravest officer in all the service in the Mysore of India.'

It was impossible to resist this appeal. I went to the door where the gentleman was waiting, and with true-heartedness expressed how great my satisfaction would be if my house could afford him any comfort.

I took him in with me to the room where my German friend was sitting. I was much pleased with the gentleness and unaffected simplicity of his manners.

He was a handsome middle-aged man – his person was robust and well-formed – his features had been originally handsome, but they were disfigured by a scar, which had materially changed their symmetry. His conversation was not distinguished by any remarkable intelligence, but after the high intellectual excitement which I had enjoyed all day with my philosophical companion, it was agreeable and gentlemanly.

Several times during supper something came across my mind as if I had seen him before, but I could neither recollect when nor where; and I observed that more than once he looked at me as if under the influence of some research in his memory. At last, I observed that his eyes were dimmed with tears, which assured me that he then recollected me. But I considered it a duty of hospitality not to inquire aught concerning him more than he was pleased to tell himself.

In the meantime, my German friend, I perceived, was watching us both, but suddenly he ceased to be interested, and appeared absorbed in thought, while good manners required me to make some efforts to entertain my guest. This led on to some inquiry concerning the scene of his services, and he told us that he had been many years in India.

'On this day eight years ago,' said he, 'I was in the battle of Borupknow, where I received the wound which has so disfigured me in the face.'

At that moment I accidentally threw my eyes upon my German friend – the look which he gave me in answer caused me to shudder from head to foot, and I began to ruminate of Nocton the recruit, and Mary Blake, while my friend continued the conversation in a light desultory manner, as it would have seemed to any stranger, but to me it was awful and oracular. He spoke to the stranger on all manner of topics, but ever and anon he brought him back, as if without design, to speak of the accidents of fortune which had befallen him of the anniversary of that day, giving it as a reason for his curious remarks that most men observe anniversaries, time and experience having taught them to notice that there were curious coincidences with respect to times, and places, and individuals – things which of themselves form part of the great demonstration of the wisdom and skill displayed in the construction, not only of the mechanical, but the mortal world, showing that each was a portion of one and the same thing.

'I have been,' said he to the stranger, 'an observer and recorder of such things. I have my book of registration here in this house; I will fetch it from my bed-chamber, and we shall see in what other things, as far as your fortunes have been concerned, how it corresponds with the accidents of your life on this anniversary.'

I observed that the stranger paled a little at this proposal, and said, with an affectation of carelessness, while he was evidently disturbed, that he would see it in the morning. But the philosopher was too intent upon his purpose to forbear. I know not what came upon me, but I urged him to bring the book. This visibly disconcerted the stranger still more, and his emotion became, as it were, a motive which induced me, in a peremptory manner, to require the production of the book, for I felt that strange horror, so often experienced, returning upon me; and was constrained, by an irresistible impulse, to seek an explanation of the circumstances by which I had for so many years suffered such an eclipse of mind.

The stranger, seeing how intent both of us were, desisted from his wish to procrastinate the curious disclosure which my friend said he could make; but it was evident he was not at ease. Indeed he was so much the reverse that when the German went for his book, he again proposed to retire, and only consented to abide at my jocular entreaty, until he should learn what his future fortunes were to be, by the truth of what would be told him of the past.

My friend soon returned with the book. It was a remarkable volume, covered with vellum, shut with three brazen clasps, secured by a lock of curious construction. Altogether it was a strange, antique, and necromantic-looking volume. The corner was studded with knobs of brass, with a small mirror in the centre, round which were inscribed in Teutonic characters words to the effect, 'I WILL SHOW THEE THYSELF'. Before unlocking the clasp, my friend gave the book to the stranger, explained some of the emblematic devices which adorned the cover, and particularly the words of the motto that surrounded the little mirror.

Whether it was from design, or that the symbols required it, the explanations of my friend were mystical and abstruse; and I could see that they produced an effect on the stranger so strong that it was evident he could with difficulty maintain his self-possession. The colour entirely faded from his countenance; he became wan and cadaverous, and his hand shook violently as he returned the volume to the philosopher, who, on receiving it back, said:

'There are things in this volume which may not be revealed to every eye, yet to those who may not discover to what they relate, they will seem trivial notations.'

He then applied the key to the lock, and unclosed the volume. My stranger guest began to breathe hard and audibly. The German turned over the vellum leaves searchingly and carefully. At last he found the record and description of my last vision, which he read aloud. It was not only minute in the main circumstances in which I had seen Nocton, but it contained an account of many things, the still life, as it is called, of the picture, which I had forgotten, and among other particulars a picturesque account of the old General whom I saw standing at the bedside.

'By all that's holy,' cried the stranger, 'it is old Cripplington himself – the queue of his hair was, as you say, always crooked, owing to a habit he had of pulling it when vexed. Where could you find the description of all this?'

I was petrified; I sat motionless as a statue, but a fearful vibration thrilled through my whole frame.

My friend looked back in his book, and found the description of my sixth vision. It contained the particulars of the crisis of battle in which, as the stranger described, he had received the wound in his face. It affected him less than the other, but still the effect upon him was impressive.

The record of the fifth vision produced a more visible alarm. The description was vivid to an extreme degree – the appearance of Nocton, sword in hand, on the rampart – the animation of the assault, and the gorgeous landscape of domes and pagodas, was limned with words as vividly as a painter could have made the scene. The stranger seemed to forget his anxiety, and was delighted with the reminiscences which the description recalled.

But when the record of the fourth vision was read, wherein Nocton was described as sitting in the regimentals of an aide-de-camp, at a convivial table, he exclaimed as if unconscious of his words:

'It was on that night I had first the honour of dining with the German general.'

The inexorable philosopher proceeded, and read what I had told him of Nocton, stretched pale and wounded on a bed, with new epaulettes spread on the coverlet, as if just unfolded from a paper. The stranger started from his seat, and cried with a hollow and fearful voice:

'This is the book of life.'

The German turned over to the second vision, which he read slowly and mournfully, especially the description of my own feelings, when I beheld the charnel visage of Mary Blake. The stranger, who had risen from his seat, and was panting with horror, cried out with a shrill howl, as it were:

'Oh that night as I was sitting in my tent, methought her spirit came and reproached me.'

I could not speak, but my German friend rose from his seat, and holding the volume in his left hand, touched it with his right, and looking sternly at the stranger, said:

'In this volume, and in your own conscience, are the evidences which prove that you are Ralph Nocton, and that on this night, twice seven years ago, you murdered Mary Blake.'

The miserable stranger lost all self-command, and cried in consternation:

'It is true, the waters raged; the rain and the hail came; she bitterly upbraided me; I flung her from the boat; the lightning flashed, and the thunder – Oh! it was not so dreadful as her drowning execrations.'

Before any answer could be given to this confession, he staggered from the spot, and almost in the same instant fell dead upon the floor.

B. W. SAVILE

Ghost stories of the American War of Independence do not seem to exist, no matter how assiduously the anthologist may search. This is partially because the short story form did not exist at the time, but the period did not seem to inspire later writers – if we put aside Shaw's *The Devil's Disciple*. To cover this period of military history the following true incidents are included in this volume; for information on non-fictitious ghostly apparitions is available for all periods of recorded history.

Bourchier Wrey Savile (1817–1888) was a divine of great learning with a talent for writing. All his books reflected his ability to examine facts and clearly evaluate his conclusions. *Apparitions*, from which the following has been extracted, is no exception and the details and cross-checks involved lead to very convincing conclusions.

5 · APPARITIONS

MR BARHAM, the well-known and popular author of *The Ingoldsby Legends*, relates the following *apparition* story in reference to the family of Dr Blomberg, the foster-brother of George IV. 'This story,' says Mr Barham, 'was repeated to me by Mr Atwood at Dr Blomberg's own table in his temporary absence. Mr Atwood declared that he had heard the story related by George IV more than once, and on one occasion when the doctor himself was present. He further stated that the King had mentioned the names of all the parties concerned, but that with exception of Major Blomberg's they had escaped his memory.' The story, with fuller explanations than those given by Mr Barham, runs as follows:

During the American war of Independence, (A.D. 1774) two officers of rank were seated in their tent awaiting the return of Major Blomberg, then absent on a foraging party, to go to supper. Their patience was well-nigh exhausted, and they were about to commence their meal, when suddenly his well-known footstep was heard approaching. Contrary, however, to their expectation, he paused at the entrance of the tent, and without coming in, called to one of them by name, requesting him with much earnestness, as soon as he returned to England, to go to a house in a certain street in

61

Westminster, and in one of the rooms, which the speaker minutely
described, he would find papers of great consequence to his son, then a
child about ten years of age. He then apparently turned away, and his
footsteps were distinctly heard retiring till their sound was lost in the
distance.

Struck with the singularity of their friend's behaviour, both officers at
once rose from the table and proceeded in search of him who had just been
speaking to them in so singular a way. A sentinel keeping his watch not
far from the tent was questioned, but denied that he had seen or heard
anyone, although, as they believed, their friend must have passed close by
his post. Shortly after their amazement was changed into a more painful
feeling by the approach of the visiting officer of the night, who informed
them that the party which went out in the morning had been surprised, and
that the dead body of poor Major Blomberg had been brought into the
camp about ten minutes before.

The two friends sought the corpse of their friend, who, as both were
fully persuaded, had addressed them at the very time when he was killed.
They found him pierced by three bullets, one of which had passed through
his temples, and must have occasioned instantaneous death.

It may easily be conceived that a careful memorandum was at once
drawn up of the request which had been made to them in so remarkable
a way by Major Blomberg, and which both the officers had so distinctly
heard. On the return of the regiment to England, no time was lost in
endeavouring to fulfil the request of their deceased friend. The house was
found without difficulty, and in a certain room, agreeably to the information which they had received in so extraordinary a manner, an old tin box
was discovered, which had been there unnoticed and unknown evidently
for a great many years, containing the title-deeds of some property in
Yorkshire, at that time held by a collateral relative of Major Blomberg,
but which eventually came into possession of his son.

There were apparently some family disputes respecting the true heir to
this property, which occasioned the audible but unseen visit of the father
to friends whom he knew would protect the interests of his orphan son.
This remarkable story happened to reach the ears of the Queen's
governess, Lady Caroline Finch, who repeated it to Her Majesty. The
Queen, feeling an interest in the child, as the foster-brother of her eldest
son, the Prince of Wales, declared that the little Blomberg should never

want a home; and immediately sending for him, ordered that he should be brought up in the royal nursery. She afterwards provided for his education, and interested herself in obtaining the settlement of the property, the claim to which had been discovered in the way related above.

When the boy had attained the age of nine years, Queen Charlotte employed Gainsborough to paint his portrait, and subsequently presented the picture to the original, who became in after years chaplain to his foster-brother George IV and canon residentiary of St Paul's Cathedral. He married Miss Floyer, a Dorsetshire lady; and having no children of his own adopted a niece of his wife, whose representative is the present possessor of the narrative, portrait, title-deeds, and estate, all of which were acquired by means of an apparition, who may be truly described as HEARD, BUT NOT SEEN.

SEEN, BUT NOT HEARD.

The scene of the present apparition story, as in that of the preceding episode, lies in America, and may therefore be not improperly described as a tale belonging to the Far West, and although that country is proverbial for its stories of the long-bow order, I venture to think, when the following evidence is placed before my readers, they will deem this as one of the best authenticated instances on record of apparitions of the dead being seen by the living.

On the 15th of October, 1785, about 4 p.m., and therefore in broad daylight, two young officers of the 33rd regiment of the line were sitting together engaged in study in a room belonging to a block house at Sydney, in the island of Cape Breton, which formed the usual quarters of officers whose regiments were serving in Canada. The room in question had two doors, one opening on an outer passage, the other into a bedroom, from which there was no exit except through the sitting-room.

These officers, who became distinguished in their profession, were subsequently known as Sir John Sherbroke* and General Wynyard.

As they were pursuing their studies, Sherbroke, happening to look up from the book he was reading, saw beside the door, which opened on the passage, the figure of a tall youth, of about twenty years of age, whose

---

* The death of one is thus announced in *Blackwood's Magazine,* for June, 1830: 'At Calverton, General Sir John Cope Sherbroke, G.C.B.' The other, General Wynyard, died Colonel of the 24th Light Dragoons, June 13th, 1809.

appearance was that of extreme emaciation. Astonished at the presence of a stranger, especially as the figure appeared clad in a light in-door costume, while they wore furs and wraps owing to the severity of the weather, Sherbroke called the attention of his companion to their unexpected visitor. 'I have often heard,' he was wont to say when subsequently relating the incident, 'of a man being as pale as death, but I never saw a living face assume the appearance of a corpse as Wynyard's did at that moment.'

Both the officers remained silently gazing at the figure as it slowly passed through the room, and entered the bed-chamber, casting on young Wynyard, as Sherbroke thought, a look of intense melancholy affection. The oppression of its presence was no sooner removed than Wynyard, grasping his friend's arm, exclaimed in a whisper, 'Why, good God, that's my brother!' 'Your brother!' replied Sherbroke, knowing that he was then in England, 'what can you mean? There must be some deception in this.' And with that he instantly rushed into the bedroom, followed by his friend. Not a soul was there! They searched in every part, until thoroughly convinced that the room was untenanted. Wynyard persisted in declaring that he had seen the apparition of his brother, while Sherbroke was inclined to regard it as a delusion, or probably a trick played by their brother-officers.

They took note of the day and hour in which the event had happened, but they resolved not to mention the occurrence in the regiment, and gradually they persuaded each other that they had been the subject of some unaccountable delusion. Nevertheless, they waited with great anxiety for letters from England, communication between the two countries being then very different in the eighteenth century, both as regards speed and regularity, from what it is now. Consequently they had to wait for a considerable length of time, during which the anxiety of Wynyard became so apparent and distressing, that his brother-officers, in spite of his resolution to the contrary, finally won from him the confession of what he had seen. The story was quickly bruited abroad, and naturally produced great excitement throughout the regiment. When the long-expected mail at length arrived, there were no letters for Wynyard, but one for Sherbroke. As soon as he had opened the packet, he beckoned his friend from the room. Expectation was at its climax during the hour in which the two friends remained closeted together. On their return to the mess-room the mystery was solved. The letter for Sherbroke was from a brother-officer in England, the first line of which read thus: 'Dear John, break to your friend Wynyard the death of his favourite brother.' He had suddenly expired on the very day, and, making due allowance for difference of latitude, at the very time, at which the friends saw the apparition in Canada.

Although it might be supposed that this solemn event would have been sufficient to have convinced Sherbroke of its truth, his mind was so strongly prepossessed against the possibility of any supernatural inter-course with the dead, that he still entertained a doubt of the report of his senses, supported as their testimony was by the coincidence of vision and fact. Some years after, however, Sherbroke had a singular confirmation of its truth. Walking one day down Piccadilly, he saw on the opposite side of the street a gentleman, whom he instantly recognized as the exact counterpart of the mysterious apparition which had been seen in Canada. Crossing over the way he accosted the stranger, and after apologizing for the intrusion, learnt that he was a Mr Hayman,* who was noted for his resemblance to the deceased officer, John Wynyard, and who affected to dress like him.

The truth of this marvellous tale of so unusual a character, compared with ordinary ghost stories, from the fact that the apparition was seen by two persons in broad daylight, one of whom had never seen the deceased party in his life, has been confirmed by a great number of persons who have investigated the matter. Some years ago Sir John Harvey, Adjutant-General of the Forces in Canada, forwarded a series of questions to Colonel Gore, of the same garrison, who was in the regiment with Sherbroke and Wynyard at the time of its occurrence, to which he replied as follows: That he was present at Sydney when the incident happened. It was at the then new barrack, which was so blocked up with ice as to have no communication with any other part of the world. He was one of the first persons who entered the room after the apparition had passed through, and, as he says, 'went into J. Wynyard's bedroom, the window of which was puttied down.' The next day he suggested to Sherbroke the propriety of making a careful memorandum of every particular connected

* It is generally thought that the party whom Sherbroke thus accosted in London was a twin-brother of John Wynyard; but Colonel Gore considered it to be the gentleman named in the text. Those who know the story of 'Martin Guerre', or its more modern prototype of 'Sir Roger', will have no difficulty in crediting the perfect resemblance which doubtless existed between John Wynyard and Hayman.

with the incident, which was then done. Colonel Gore adds: 'I remember on the 6th of June our first letters from England brought the news of John Wynyard's death (which had happened) on the very night they saw his *apparition*.'

Captain Harvey Scott, RN, who was Assistant Surveyor of Nova Scotia about fifty years ago, when Sir John Sherbroke was Governor of that province, used to relate, when residing at Blackheath, that on one occasion at a state dinner party at the Governor's table, a guest happened to remark that a newspaper, just received from England, contained a most extraordinary ghost story, in which His Excellency's name appeared. Whereupon Sir John Sherbroke, with much emotion, quickly replied, 'I earnestly beg that the subject may not be again mentioned.' The impression on the minds of the company being that he considered the matter too awful to be talked about again on such an occasion.

Captain Harvey Scott subsequently wrote to Mr Robert Owen, the United States Ambassador at the court of Naples, the following account of what he had heard on the subject: 'About six years ago, dining alone with my dear friend, now gone to his account, General Paul Anderson, CB, I related to him the story of Wynyard's apparition, in substance exactly as you have it. When I had finished, "It is extraordinary enough," said he, "that you have related the story almost *verbatim* as I heard it from Sir John Sherbroke's own lips a short time before his death." (May, 1830.) I asked the General whether Sir John expressed any opinion about the incident. "Yes," he replied, "he assured me in the most solemn manner that he believed the appearance to have been a ghost or spirit; and added that this belief was shared by his friend Wynyard." General Anderson was a distinguished Peninsular war officer, a major under Sir John Moore, and one of those who assisted to bury that gallant general.'

I would only add, that this remarkable story, which has been investigated by so many persons,* affords as clear an instance of the truth of an *apparition* of the dead as it is possible for the mind to conceive.

THE SIEGE OF LUCKNOW

Anyone who can refer to a file of *The Times* may read in that journal of December 29th, 1857, the following announcement:

* See also *Letters on the Truths contained in Popular Superstitions*, by Herbert Mayo, MD Ed. Frankfort, 1849, p. 62.

'The following telegram was received at the East India House yesterday morning: The Commander-in-Chief, (Sir Colin Campbell, afterwards Lord Clyde,) entered Oude on the 9th inst. (November.) On the 13th he commenced operations by blowing-up the fort of Jhullawau, near the Alumbagh; on the 15th he occupied Dilkhoosha Park and Martinere, after a running fight of two hours. Our loss is small; Lieutenant Mayne, Horse Artillery, and *Lieutenant Wheatcroft, Carbineers, killed.*'

The Bombay correspondent of *The Times* adds: 'On Sunday, the 15th, (Of November,) the Commander-in-Chief marched across the country to the house and park of *Dilkhoosha*, "Heart's Delight," which was carried by Sir Colin after a running fight of two hours – the operations of the day, during which the English loss in officers had been Lieutenants Mayne, of the Quartermaster-General's department, and *Wheatcroft* of the Carbineers, came to an end.'

Notwithstanding the above statement from the official Gazette of the Commander-in-Chief, backed up by the supposed accuracy of *The Times* newspaper, it is quite certain, as we shall be able presently to show, that the regiment of 'Carabiniers,' as it is more correctly spelt in the *Army List*, was not at the siege of Lucknow, nor ever near it; that there was no 'Lieutenant' of the name of *Wheatcroft* belonging to that corps, as the officer of that name is twice represented; and that he was not killed on 'Sunday, November 15th, 1857,' as he is stated to have been, all of which we shall proceed to prove by the following extraordinary tale.

The facts connected with the *apparition* which we are about to relate are these. By the *Army List* of March, 1857, it appears that Captain (not Lieutenant) Wheatcroft was an officer in the 6th Dragoons, which regiment was known by the name of 'The Inniskillings'. In July, 1857, he exchanged into the 6th Dragoon Guards, called 'The Carabiniers', which has been a good deal before the public of late in consequence of its having been the regiment to which the noted 'Sir Roger' is said to have belonged. In September of the same year Captain Wheatcroft sailed from England to join his regiment, then quartered at Meerut, where the Indian Mutiny commenced on the memorable Sunday, May 10th, of that year. And the *Army List* of January 29th, 1858, contains an entry, 'Captain German Wheatcroft killed in action, November 15th, 1857.'

Mrs German Wheatcroft did not accompany her husband to India, but remained in England, residing with her mother at Cambridge. On

Saturday night, November 14th, (it is necessary to note the exact dates,) she dreamed that she saw her husband looking anxious and ill, upon which she awoke naturally much agitated. It was bright moonlight; and on looking up, what was her horror at seeing the same figure that had appeared in her dream standing close by her bedside. He appeared dressed in his uniform, the hands pressed across the breast, his hair dishevelled, and his face deadly pale. His large dark eyes were fondly and mournfully fixed upon her, their expression was that of great excitement, and there was a peculiar contraction of the mouth, which was common to him when agitated. She detected each particular of his dress, as distinctly as she had ever done in her life; and she remarked having noticed between his hands the white of his shirt bosom, unstained apparently with blood. The *apparition* seemed to bend forward as if in much pain, and to make an effort to speak; but there was no sound. It remained visible about sixty seconds, and then silently vanished away.

The first idea of the poor bereaved wife was to ascertain if she was actually awake. She rubbed her eyes with the sheet, and felt that the touch was real. Her little nephew was in bed with her; she bent over the sleeping child and listened to its breathing – the sound was distinct: she became convinced that what she had seen was no dream; and it need not be added that she could obtain no more sleep on that night.

On the following morning she told her mother what had occurred a few hours before, expressing at the same time her strong conviction – though she had not noticed any marks of blood on his dress – that her husband must have been either killed or grievously wounded. And so fully impressed was she with this thought, and the reality of the apparition she had seen, that she positively declined all parties, notwithstanding the entreaties of her friends, declaring that, uncertain whether she was not already a widow, she would remain at home until she had received tidings of her husband (if he was still alive) of a later date than the 14th November.

We have already seen that the telegram announcing the fate of Captain German Wheatcroft was published in *The Times* of December 29th, 1857, stating that he was killed before Lucknow on the *fifteenth* of November. The sad intelligence attracted the attention of Mr Wilkinson, a London solicitor, who had charge of Captain Wheatcroft's affairs. When he subsequently met the widow on business, she informed him that she 'had been quite prepared for the melancholy news, but that she was quite convinced her husband could not have been killed on the *fifteenth* of November, as the official despatch stated, inasmuch as she had seen his *apparition* on the night of the *fourteenth*.' Allowing for the difference of longitude between London and Lucknow as about five hours, midnight of the 14th in England would synchronize with 5 a.m. of the 15th in India. But it was in the *afternoon* of the 15th in India, according to Sir Colin Campbell's despatch, that Captain Wheatcroft is represented as having been killed; and therefore the *apparition*, which stood by the bedside of Mrs Wheatcroft on the night of the 14th in England, must have been by her several hours before the engagement in which he fell had taken place, and while he was still alive!

It was necessary for Mr Wilkinson to apply to the War Office for the official certificate of his client's death; and the return which he received in reply to his application was worded as follows:

'No. $\frac{9579}{1}$ War Office, January 30th, 1858.

'These are to certify that it appears by the records in this office, that Captain German Wheatcroft, of the 6th Dragoon Guards, was killed in action on November 15th, 1857.

'(Signed) B. HAWES.'

While Mr Wilkinson's mind remained in a great state of uncertainty as to the exact date of Captain Wheatcroft's death, on account of the conflicting evidence between Mrs Wheatcroft and the War Office, a remarkable incident occurred, which seemed to cast further suspicion on the accuracy of both the telegram and the official records, and to confirm in no slight degree the evidence of the widow from the apparition she had seen.

Happening one evening to be paying a visit to some friends – the Rev Mr Nenner, Professor of Hebrew at the Independent College in St John's Wood, London, and his wife – Mr Wilkinson related to them as an extraordinary circumstance the apparition which Mrs German Wheatcroft had seen of her husband, and described the figure as it had appeared to her at Cambridge; upon which Mrs Nenner, turning to her husband, observed, 'Why that must be the very person I saw that evening we were talking about India, when you were drawing a picture of an elephant with a howdah on his back. Mr Wilkinson has described his exact position and appearance – the uniform of a British officer, his hands pressed across his

F

breast, his form bent forward as if in great pain. The figure appeared just behind my husband, looking over his left shoulder.'

'Did you attempt to obtain any communication from the apparition?' asked Mr Wilkinson.

'Yes; we procured one through the medium of my husband.'*

'Can you recollect what it was?' asked Mr Wilkinson.

'It was to the effect that he had been killed in India that afternoon by a wound in the breast; and adding, as I distinctly remember, these words: *"That thing I used to go about in is not buried yet."* I particularly remarked the expression.'

'When did this happen?'

'About 9 p.m. several weeks ago; but I do not recollect the exact date.'

'Can you not call to mind,' asked Mr Wilkinson, 'something that would enable you to fix the exact day?'

Mrs Nenner reflected for a few minutes, and then said, 'I remember nothing except that, while my husband was drawing and I was talking to a lady who had called to see us, a servant brought in a bill for some German vinegar, and that as I recommended it being superior to English, we had a bottle brought for inspection.'

'Did you pay the bill?'

'Yes: I recollect sending out the money by the servant.'

'Was the bill receipted?'

'I suppose so; but I can soon see.'

Mrs Nenner quickly found the bill; and on looking it over, the receipt bore the date of the *fourteenth* of November!

This remarkable confirmation of Mrs German Wheatcroft's conviction as to the day of her husband's death produced such an impression on Mr Wilkinson that he called at the office of the well-known army agents, Cox and Greenwood, to ascertain if there was any mistake in the certificate. Nothing there disclosed any sign of inaccuracy, but the reverse; for Captain Wheatcroft's death was mentioned *in two separate despatches* of Sir Colin Campbell; and in both instances the date corresponded with that given in the telegram.

So matters rested until the following March, when the family of Captain

---

* It is necessary to explain that Mr and Mrs Nenner are supporters of the system called 'Spiritualism'. I abstain from expressing any opinion on that singular phenomenon; I merely desire to record facts.

German Wheatcroft received a letter from Captain Godfrey Cooper, an officer belonging to the Military Train Corps, dated Lucknow, December 19th, 1857, informing them that Captain German Wheatcroft had been killed before Lucknow while gallantly charging with the Military Train *on the afternoon of the fourteenth of November*, and not on the day following, as erroneously reported in the telegram, the official despatches of Sir Colin Campbell, and the records of the War Office. Captain Wheatcroft was not serving with his own regiment, the Carabiniers, which was then quartered at Meerut. Immediately on arriving at Cawnpore he had volunteered his services, which were at first declined, but subsequently accepted; and he joined the Military Train then starting for Lucknow; and in their ranks, as Byron says of Bruswick's fated chieftain –

'He rushed into the field, and fighting foremost fell.'

Captain Godfrey Cooper was riding close beside him when he was struck by the fragment of a shell in the breast, and never spoke after he was hit. He was buried in the Dilkoosha; and there may be seen to this day the little wooden cross erected by his friend, Lieutenant Rich, of the 9th Lancers, at the head of his grave, on which are cut the initial letters, 'G.W.', with the date of his death, November 14th, 1857.

After the lapse of more than a year, the War Office made the proper correction as to the date of Captain Wheatcroft's death; for Mr Wilkinson having occasion, as solicitor for the estate of the deceased officer, to apply for a *second* copy of the certificate in April, 1859, found it in exactly the same words of those already given, save that the 14th of November was substituted for the 15th.

This is probably the only instance on record where an *apparition* has proved the means of correcting an erroneous date in the official despatch of a General Commanding-in-Chief. It is also valuable as furnishing the very rare example of the same *apparition* appearing to two different parties on the same night in England shortly after Captain Wheatcroft had been killed in battle in India; for, supposing he fell on the afternoon of the 14th in India, it was within a few hours *after* that he appeared to two different parties in England. Nor can it be alleged that the narrative related by one caused the apparition of the same figure to the other. For Mrs German Wheatcroft was at the same time at Cambridge, while Mrs Nenner on the same night was in London; and it was not until weeks after the occurrence that either knew what the other had seen.

JAMES GRANT

According to Sir Winston Churchill the invasion of Britain by Prince Charles Edward Stuart was 'one of the most audacious and irresponsible enterprises in British history'. Charles landed in the Western Isles in June, 1745, was successful at first, but almost a year later was in retreat. 'A winter march began to the fastness of Northern Scotland. The English forces followed like vultures, hanging upon the rear and wings of the rebel army. Murray showed great skill in the withdrawal, and in the rearguard actions his troops were invariably successful. They turned and mauled their pursuers at Falkirk. But with Teutonic thoroughness the Duke of Cumberland concentrated the English armies for a decision, and in April, 1746, on Culloden Moor the last chances of a Stuart restoration were swept into the past forever. . . . No quarter was given on the battlefield, where Cumberland earned his long-lived title of "Butcher".'

James Grant (1822–1887) was the son of an army captain and, because his mother died when he was young, lived with him when serving in Canada. James served as an Ensign from 1840 to 1843 but established himself as a military expert who was often consulted by the War Office. He was a prolific military novelist and his works accurately reflect life as it was lived in the armed forces at that time. *The Phantom Regiment* is a unique story of horror arising from the greater horror of the Battle of Culloden.

6 · THE PHANTOM REGIMENT

In their younger days Meinie and her gudeman had been lovers – lovers as a boy and girl – but were separated by poverty, and then Ewen Mac Ewen enlisted as a soldier, in the 26th Cameronian Regiment, with which he saw some sharp service in the West Indies and America. The light-hearted young highlander became, in time, a grave, stern, and morose soldier, with the most rigid ideas of religious deportment and propriety: for this distinguished Scottish regiment was of Puritan origin, being one of those raised among the Westland Covenanters, after the deposition of King James VII by the Estates of Scotland. England surrendered to William of Orange without striking a blow; but the defence of Dunkeld, and the victorious battle of Killycrankie, ended the northern campaign, in which the noble Dundee was slain, and the army of the cavaliers dispersed.

The Cameronian Regiment introduced their sectarian forms, their rigorous discipline, and plain mode of public worship into their own ranks, and so strict was their code of morals, that even the Non-jurors and Jacobins admitted the excellence and stern propriety of their bearing. They left the Scottish Service for the British, at the Union, in 1707, but still wear on their appointments the five-pointed star, which was the armorial bearing of the colonel who embodied them; and, moreover, retain the privilege of supplying their own regimental Bibles.

After many years of hard fighting in the old 26th, and after carrying a halberd in the kilted regiment of the Isles, Ewen Mac Ewen returned home to his native place, the great plain of Moray, a graver, and, in bearing, a sadder man than when he left it.

His first inquiry was for Meinie.

She had married a rival of his, twenty years ago.

'God's will be done,' sighed Ewen, as he lifted his bonnet, and looked upwards.

He built himself a little cottage, in the old highland fashion, in his native strath, at a sunny spot, where the Uise Nairn – the Water of Alders – flowed in front, and a wooded hill arose behind. He hung his knapsack above the fireplace; deposited his old and sorely thumbed regimental Bible (with the Cameronian star on its boards), and the tin case containing his colonel's letter recommending him to the minister, and the discharge, which gave sixpence per diem as the reward of sixteen battles – all on the shelf of the little window, which contained three panes of glass, with a yoke in the centre of each, and there he settled himself down in peace, to plant his own kail, knit his own hose, and to make his own kilts, a grave and thoughtful but contented old fellow, awaiting the time, as he said, 'when the Lord would call him away'.

Now it chanced that a poor widow, with several children, built herself a little thatched house on the opposite side of the drove road – an old Fingalian path – which ascended the pastoral glen; and the ready-handed veteran lent his aid to thatch it, and to sling her kail-pot on the cruicks, and was wont thereafter to drop in of an evening to smoke his pipe, to tell old stories of the storming of Ticonderoga, and to ask her little ones the catechism and biblical questions. Within a week or so, he discovered that the widow was Meinie – the ripe, blooming Meinie of other years – an old, a faded, and a sad-eyed woman now; and poor Ewen's lonely heart swelled within him, as he thought of all that had passed since last they met, and as he spake of what they were, and what they might have been, had fate been kind, or fortune roved more true.

We have heard much about the hidden and mysterious principle of affinity, and more about the sympathy and sacredness that belong to a first and early love; well, the heart of the tough old Cameronian felt these gentle impulses, and Meinie was no stranger to them. They were married, and for fifteen years, there was no happier couple on the banks of the Nairn. Strange to say, they died on the same day, and were interred in the ancient burying-ground of Dalcross, where now they lie, near the ruined walls of the old vicarage kirk of the Catholic times. God rest them in their humble highland graves!

In process of time the influx of French and English tourists who came to visit the country of the clans, and to view the plain of Culloden, after the publication of *Waverley* gave to all Britain, that which we name in Scotland 'the tartan fever', and caused the old path which passed the cot of Ewen to become a turnpike road; a tollbar – that most obnoxious of all impositions to a Celt – was placed across the mouth of the little glen, barring the way directly to the battlefield; and of this gate the old pensioner Ewen naturally became keeper; and during the summer season, when, perhaps, a hundred carriages per day rolled through, it became a source of revenue alike to him, and to the Lord of Cawdor and the Laird of Kilravok, the road trustees. And the chief pleasure of Ewen's existence was to sit on a thatched seat by the gate, for then he felt conscious of being in office – on duty – a species of sentinel; and it smacked of the old time when the Generale was beaten in the morning, and the drums rolled tattoo at night; when he had belts to pipe-clay, and boots to blackball; when there were wigs to frizzle and queues to tie, and to be all trim and in order to meet Monseigneur le Marquis de Montcalm, or General Washington 'right early in the morning', and there by the new barrier of the glen Ewen sat the live-long day, with spectacles on nose, and the Cameronian Bible on his knee, as he spelled his way through Deuteronomy and tribes of Judah.

Slates in due time replaced the green thatch of his little cottage; then a diminutive additional storey, with two small dormer windows, was added thereto, and the thrifty Meinie placed a paper in her window informing shepherds, the chance wayfarers, and the wandering deer-stalkers that she had a room to let; but summer passed away, the sportsman forsook the brown scorched mountains, the gay tourist ceased to come north, and the advertisement turned from white to yellow, and from yellow to flyblown green in her window; the winter snows descended on the hills, the pines stood in long and solemn ranks by the white frozen Nairn, but 'the room upstairs' still remained without a tenant.

Anon the snow passed away, the river again flowed free, the flowers began to bloom; the young grass to sprout by the hedgerows, and the mavis to sing on the fauld-dykes, for spring was come again, and joyous summer soon would follow; and one night – it was the 26th April – Ewen was exhibiting his penmanship in large text-hand by preparing the new announcement of 'a room to let', when he paused, and looked up as a peal of thunder rumbled across the sky; a red gleam of lightning flashed in the darkness without, and then they heard the roar of the deep broad Nairn, as its waters, usually so sombre and so slow, swept down from the wilds of Badenoch, flooded with the melting snow of the past winter.

A dreadful storm of thunder, rain, and wind came on, and the little cottage rocked on its foundations; frequently the turf-fire upon the hearth was almost blown about the clay-floor, by the downward gusts that bellowed in the chimney. The lightning gleamed incessantly, and seemed to play about the hill of Urchany and the ruins of Caistel Fionlah; the woods groaned and creaked, and the trees seemed to shriek as their strong limbs were torn asunder by the gusts which in some places laid side by side the green sapling of last summer, and the old oak that had stood for a thousand years – that had seen Macbeth and Duncan ride from Nairn, and had outlived the wars of the Comyns and the Clanchattan.

The swollen Nairn tore down its banks, and swept trees, rocks, and stones in wild confusion to the sea, mingling the pines of Aberarder with the old oaks of Cawdor; while the salt spray from the Moray Firth was swept seven miles inland, where it encrusted with salt the trees, the houses, and windows, and whatever it fell on as it mingled with the ceaseless rain, while deep, hoarse, and loud the incessant thunder rattled across the sky, 'as if all the cannon on earth,' according to Ewen, 'were exchanging salvoes between Urchany and the Hill of Geddes.'

Meinie grew pale, and sat with a finger on her mouth, and a startled expression in her eyes, listening to the uproar without; four children, two of whom were Ewen's, and her last addition to the clan, clung to her skirts.

Ewen had just completed the invariable prayer and chapter for the night, and was solemnly depositing his old regimental companion, with *Baxter's Saints' Rest*, in a place of security, when a tremendous knock – a knock that rang above the storm – shook the door of the cottage.

'Who can this be, and in such a night?' said Meinie.

'The Lord knoweth,' responded Ewen gravely, 'but he knocks both loud and late.'

'Inquire before you open,' urged Meinie, seizing her husband's arm, as the impatient knock was renewed with treble violence.

'Who comes there?' demanded Ewen, in a soldierly tone.

'A friend,' replied a strange voice without, and in the same manner.

'What do you want?'

'Fire and smoke!' cried the other, giving the door a tremendous kick; 'do you ask that in such a devil of a night as this? You have a room to let, have you not?'

'Yes.'

'Well; open the door, or blood and 'oons I'll bite your nose off!'

Ewen hastened to undo the door; and then, all wet and dripping as if he had just been fished up from the Moray Firth, there entered a strange-looking old fellow in a red coat; he stumped vigorously on a wooden leg, and carried on his shoulders a box, which he flung down with a crash that shook the dwelling, saying,

'There – damn you – I have made good my billet at last.'

'So it seems,' said Ewen, reclosing the door in haste to exclude the tempest, lest his house should be unroofed and torn asunder.

'Harkee, comrade, what garrison or fortress is this,' asked the visitor, 'that peaceable folks are to be challenged in this fashion, and forced to give parole and countersign before they march in – eh?'

'It is my house, comrade; and so you had better keep a civil tongue in your head.'

'Civil tongue? Fire and smoke, you mangy cur! I can be as civil as my neighbours; but get me a glass of grog, for I am as wet as we were the night before Minden.'

'Where have you come from in such a storm as this?'

'Where you'd not like to go – so never mind; but, grog, I tell you – get me some grog, and a bit of tobacco; it is long since I tasted either.'

Ewen hastened to get a large quaigful of stiff Glenlivat, which the veteran drained to his health, and that of Meinie; but first he gave them a most diabolical grin, and threw into the liquor some black stuff saying,

'I always mix my grog with gunpowder – it's a good tonic; I learned that of a comrade who fell at Minden on the glorious 1st of August, '59.'

'You have been a soldier, then?'

'Right! I was one of the 25th, or old Edinburgh Regiment; they enlisted me, though an Englishman, I believe; for my good old dam was a follower of the camp.'

'Our number was 26th – the old Cameronian Regiment – so we were near each other, you see, comrade.'

'Nearer than you would quite like, mayhap,' said Wooden-leg, with another grin and a dreadful oath.

'And you have served in Germany?' asked Ewen.

'Germany – aye, and marched over every foot of it, from Hanover to Hell, and back again. I have fought in Flanders, too.'

'I wish you had come a wee while sooner,' said Ewen gravely, for this discourse startled his sense of propriety.

'Sooner,' snarled this shocking old fellow, who must have belonged to that army 'which swore so terribly in Flanders', as good Uncle Toby says; 'sooner – for what?'

'To have heard me read a chapter, and to have joined us in prayer.'

'Prayers be d—ned!' cried the other, with a shout of laughter, and a face expressive of fiendish mockery, as he gave his wooden leg a thundering blow on the floor; 'fire and smoke – another glass of grog – and then we'll settle about my billet upstairs.'

While getting another dram, which hospitality prevented him from refusing, Ewen scrutinized this strange visitor, whose aspect and attire were very remarkable; but wholly careless of what anyone thought, he sat by the hearth, wringing his wet wig, and drying it at the fire.

He was a little man, of a spare, but strong and active figure, which indicated great age; his face resembled that of a rat; behind it hung a long queue that waved about like a pendulum when he moved his head, which was quite bald, and smooth as a cricket-ball, save where a long and livid scar – evidently a sword cut – traversed it. This was visible while he sat drying his wig; but as that process was somewhat protracted, he uttered an oath, and thrust his cocked hat on one side of his head, and very much over his left eye, which was covered by a patch. This head-dress was the old military triple-cocked hat, bound with yellow braid, and having on one side the hideous black leather cockade of the House of Hanover, now happily disused in the British army, and retained as a badge of service by liverymen alone. His attire was an old threadbare red coat, faced with yellow, having square tails and deep cuffs, with braided holes; he wore knee-breeches on his spindle shanks, one of which terminated, as I have said, in a wooden pin; he carried a large knotted stick; and, in outline and aspect, very much resembled, as Ewen thought, Frederick the Great of Prussia, or an old Chelsea pensioner, or the soldiers he had seen delineated in antique prints of the Flemish wars. His solitary orb possessed a most diabolical leer, and, whichever way you turned, it seemed to regard you with the fixed glare of a basilisk.

'You are a stranger hereabout, I presume?' said Ewen drily.

'A stranger now, certainly; but I was pretty well known in this locality once. There are some bones buried hereabout that may remember me,' he replied, with a grin that showed his fangless jaws.

'Bones!' reiterated Ewen, aghast.

'Yes, bones – Culloden Muir lies close by here, does it not?'

'It does – then you have travelled this road before?'

'Death and the Devil! I should think so, comrade; on this very night sixty years ago I marched along this road, from Nairn to Culloden, with the army of His Royal Highness, the Great Duke of Cumberland, Captain-General of the British troops, in pursuit of the rebels under the Popish Pretender –'

'Under His Royal Highness Prince Charles, you mean, comrade,' said Ewen, in whose breast – Cameronian though he was – a tempest of Highland wrath and loyalty swelled up at these words.

'Prince – ha! ha! ha!' laughed the other; 'had you said as much then, the gallows had been your doom. Many a man I have shot, and many a boy I have brained with the butt end of my musket, for no other crime than wearing the tartan, even as you this night wear it.'

Ewen made a forward stride as if he would have taken the wicked boaster by the throat; his anger was kindled to find himself in presence of a veritable soldier of the infamous 'German Butcher', whose merciless massacre of the wounded clansmen and their defenceless families will never be forgotten in Scotland while oral tradition and written record exist; but Ewen paused, and said in his quiet way,

'Blessed be the Lord! these times and things have passed away from the land, to return to it no more. We are both old men now; by your own reckoning, you must at least have numbered fourscore years, and in that, you are by twenty my better man. You are my guest tonight, moreover, so we must not quarrel, comrade. My father was killed at Culloden.'

'On which side?'

'The right one – for he fell by the side of old Keppoch, and his last words were, "Righ Hamish gu Bragh!" '

'Fire and smoke!' laughed the old fellow, 'I remember these things as if they only happened yesterday – mix me some more grog and put it in the bill – I was the company's butcher in those days – it suited my taste – so when I was not stabbing and slashing the sheep and cattle of the rascally commissary, I was cutting the throats of the Scots and French, for there were plenty of them, and Irish too, who fought against the King's troops in Flanders. We had hot work, that day at Culloden – hotter than at Minden, where we fought in heavy marching order, with our blankets, kettles, and provisions, on a broiling noon, when the battlefield was cracking under a blazing sun, and the whole country was sweltering like the oven of the Great Baker.'

'Who is he?'

'What! you don't know him? Ha! ha! ha! Ho! ho! ho! come, that is good.'

Ewen expostulated with the boisterous old fellow on this style of conversation, which, as you may easily conceive, was very revolting to the prejudices of a well-regulated Cameronian soldier.

'Come, come, you old devilskin,' cried the other, stirring up the fire with his wooden leg, till the sparks flashed and gleamed like his solitary eye; 'you may as well sing psalms to a dead horse as preach to me. Hark how the thunder roars, like the great guns at Carthagena. More grog – put it in the bill – or, halt, d—me! pay yourself,' and he dashed on the table a handful of silver of the reigns of George II and the Glencoe assassin, William of Orange.

He obtained more whiskey, and drank it raw, seasoning it from time to time with gunpowder, just as an Arab does his cold water with ginger.

'Where did you lose your eye, comrade?'

'At Culloden; but I found the fellow who pinked me, next day, as he lay bleeding on the field; he was a Cameron, in a green velvet jacket, all covered with silver; so I stripped off his lace, as I had seen my mother do, and then I brained him with the butt-end of brown-bess – and before his wife's eyes, too! What the deuce do you growl at, comrade? Such things will happen in war, and you know that orders must be obeyed. My eye was gone – but it was the left one, and I was saved the trouble of closing it when taking aim. This slash on the sconce I got at the battle of Preston Pans, from the Celt who slew Colonel Gardiner.'

'The Celt was my father – the Miller of Invernahyle,' said Meinie, proudly.

'Your father! fire and smoke! do you say so? His hand was a heavy one!' cried Wooden-leg, while his eye glowed like the orb of a hyena.

'And your leg?'

'I lost at Minden, in Kingsley's Brigade, comrade; aye, my leg d—n! – that was indeed a loss.'

'A warning to repentance, I would say.'

'Then you would say wrong. Ugh! I remember when the shot – a twelve-pounder – took me just as we were rushing with charged bayonets on the French cannoniers. Smash! my leg was gone, and I lay sprawling and bleeding in a ploughed field near the Weser, while my comrades swept over me with a wild hurrah! the colours waving, and drums beating a charge.'

'And what did you do?'

'I lay there and swore, believe me.'

'That would not restore your limb again.'

'No; but a few hearty oaths relieve the mind; and the mind relieves the body; you understand me, comrade; so there I lay all night under a storm of rain like this, bleeding and sinking; afraid of the knives of the plundering death-hunters, for my mother had been one, and I remembered well how she looked after the wounded, and cured them of their agony.'

'Was your mother one of those infer –' began Mac Ewen.

'Don't call her hard names now, comrade; she died on the day after the defeat at Val; with the Provost Marshal's cord round her neck – a cordon less ornamental than that of St Louis.'

'And your father?'

'Was one of Howard's Regiment; but which the devil only knows, for it was a point on which the old lady, honest woman, had serious doubts herself.'

'After the loss of your leg, of course you left the service?'

'No, I became the company's butcher; but, fire and smoke, get me another glass of grog; take a share yourself, and don't sit staring at me like a Dutch Souterkin conceived of a winter night over a *pot de feu*, as all the world knows King William was. Damn! let us be merry together – ha, ha, ha! ho, ho, ho! and I'll sing you a song of the old whig times.'

And while he continued to rant and sing, he beat time with his wooden leg, and endeavoured to outroar the stormy wind and the hiss of the drenching rain. Even Mac Ewen, though he was an old soldier, felt some uneasiness, and Meinie trembled in her heart, while the children clung to her skirts and hid their little faces, as if this singing, riot, and jollity were impious at such a time, when the awful thunder was ringing its solemn peals across the midnight sky.

Although this strange old man baffled or parried every inquiry of Ewen as to whence he had come, and how and why he wore that antiquated uniform, on his making a lucrative offer to take the upper room of the little toll-house for a year – exactly a year – when Ewen thought of his poor pension of sixpence per diem, of their numerous family, and Meinie now becoming old and requiring many little comforts, all scruples were overcome by the pressure of necessity, and the mysterious old soldier was duly installed in the attic, with his corded chest, scratch-wig, and wooden-leg; moreover, he paid the first six month's rent in advance, dashing the money – which was all coin of the first and second Georges, on the table with a bang and an oath, swearing that he disliked being indebted to any man.

The next morning was calm and serene; the green hills lifted their heads into the blue placid sky. There was no mist on the mountains, nor rain in the valley. The flood in the Nairn had subsided, though its waters were still muddy and perturbed; but save this, and the broken branches that strewed the wayside – with an uprooted tree, or a paling laid flat on the ground, there was no trace of yesterday's hurricane, and Ewen heard Wooden-leg (he had no other name for his new lodger) stumping about overhead, as the old fellow left his bed betimes, and after trimming his queue and wig, pipeclaying his yellow facings and beating them well with the brush, in a soldier-like way, he descended to breakfast, but, disdaining porridge and milk, broiled salmon and bannocks of barley-meal, he called for a can of stiff grog, mixed it with powder from his wide waistcoat pocket, and drank it off at a draught. Then he imperiously desired Ewen to take his bonnet and staff, and accompany him so far as Culloden, 'because,' said he, 'I have come a long, long way to see the old place again.'

Wooden-leg seemed to gather – what was quite unnecessary to him – new life, vigour, and energy – as they traversed the road that led to the battlefield, and felt the pure breeze of the spring morning blowing on their old and wrinkled faces.

The atmosphere was charmingly clear and serene. In the distance lay the spires of Inverness, and the shining waters of the Moray Firth, studded with sails, and the ramparts of Fort George were seen jutting out at the termination of a long and green peninsula. In the foreground stood the castle of Dalcross, raising its square outline above a wood, which terminates the eastern side of the landscape. The pine-clad summit of Dun Daviot incloses the west, while on every hand between, stretched the dreary moor of Drummossie – the Plain of Culloden – whilom drenched in the blood of Scotland's bravest hearts.

Amid the purple heath lie two or three grass-covered mounds.

These are the graves of the dead – the graves of the loyal Highlanders, who fell on that disastrous field, and of the wounded, who were so mercilessly murdered next day by an order of Cumberland, which he pencilled on the back of a card (the Nine of Diamonds); thus they were dispatched by platoons, stabbed by bayonets, slashed by sword and spontoons, or brained by the butt end of musket and carbine; officers and men were to be seen emulating each other in this scene of cowardice and cold-blooded atrocity, which filled every camp and barrack in Continental Europe with scorn at the name of an English soldier.

Ewen was a Highlander, and his heart filled with such thoughts as these, when he stood by the grassy tombs where the fallen brave are buried with the hopes of the house they died for; he took off his bonnet and stood bare-headed, full of sad and silent contemplation; while his garrulous companion viewed the field with his single eye, that glowed like a hot coal, and pirouetted on his wooden pin in a very remarkable manner, as he surveyed on every side the scene of that terrible encounter, where, after enduring a long cannonade of round shot and grape, the Highland swordsmen, chief and gillie, the noble and the nameless, flung themselves with reckless valour on the ranks of those whom they had already routed in two pitched battles.

'It was an awful day,' said Ewen, in a low voice, but with a gleam in his grey Celtic eye; 'yonder my father fell wounded; the bullet went through his shield and pierced him here, just above the belt; he was living next day, when my mother – a poor wailing woman with a babe at her breast – found him; but an officer of Barrel's Regiment ran a sword twice through his body and killed him; for the orders of the German Duke were, "that no quarter should be given". This spring is named MacGillivray's Well, because here they butchered the dying chieftain who led the MacIntoshes – aye bayonetted him, next day at noon, in the arms of his bonnie young wife and his pair auld mother! The inhumane monsters! I have been a soldier,' continued Ewen, 'and I have fought for my country; but had I stood that day on this Moor of Culloden, I would have shot the German Butcher, the coward who fled from Flanders – I would by the God who hears me, though that moment had been my last!'

'Ha, ha, ha! Ho, ho, ho!' rejoined his queer companion. 'It seems like yesterday since I was here; I don't see many changes, except that the dead are all buried, whereas we left them to the crows, and a carriage-road has been cut across the field, just where we seized some women, who were looking among the dead for their husbands, and who –'

'Well?'

Wooden-leg whistled, and gave Ewen a diabolical leer with his snaky eye, as he resumed,

'I see the ridge where the clans formed line – every tribe with its chief in front, and his colours in the centre, when we, hopeless of victory, and thinking only of defeat, approached them; and I can yet see standing the old stone wall which covered their right flank. Fire and smoke! it was against that wall we placed the wounded, when we fired at them by platoons next day. I finished some twenty rebels there myself.'

Ewen's hand almost caught the haft of his skenedhu, as he said, hoarsely,

'Old man, do not call them rebels in my hearing, and least of all by the graves where they lie; they were good men and true; if they were in error, they have long since answered to God for it, even as we one day must answer; therefore let us treat their memory with respect, as soldiers should ever treat their brothers in arms who fall in war.'

But Wooden-leg laughed with his strange eldritch yell, and then they returned together to the tollhouse in the glen; but Ewen felt strongly dissatisfied with his lodger, whose conversation was so calculated to shock alike his Jacobitical and his religious prejudices. Every day this sentiment grew stronger, and he soon learned to deplore in his inmost heart having ever accepted the rent, and longed for the time when he should be rid of him, but, at the end of the six months, Wooden-leg produced the rent for the remainder of the year, still in old silver of the two first Georges, with a few Spanish dollars, and swore he would set the house on fire if Ewen made any more apologies about their inability to make him sufficiently comfortable and so forth; for his host and hostess had resorted to every pretence and expedient to rid themselves of him handsomely.

But Wooden-leg was inexorable.

He had bargained for his billet for a year; he had paid for it; and a year he would stay, though the Lord Justice General of Scotland himself should say nay!

Boisterous and authoritative, he awed everyone by his terrible gimlet eye and the volleys of oaths with which he overwhelmed them on suffering the smallest contradiction; thus he became the terror of all; and shepherds crossed the hills by the most unfrequented routes rather than pass the toll-bar, where they vowed that his eye bewitched their sheep and cattle. To every whispered and stealthy inquiry as to where his lodger had come from, and how or why he had thrust himself upon this lonely tollhouse, Ewen could only groan and shrug his shoulders, or reply,

'He came on the night of the hurricane, like a bird of evil omen; but on the twenty-sixth of April we will be rid of him, please Heaven! It is close at hand, and he shall march then, sure as my name is Ewen Mac Ewen!'

He seemed to be troubled in his conscience, too, or to have strange visitors; for often in stormy nights he was heard swearing or threatening, and expostulating; and once or twice, when listening at the foot of the stair, Ewen heard him shouting and conversing from his window with persons on the road, although the bar was shut, locked, and there was no one visible there.

On another windy night, Ewen and his wife were scared by hearing Wooden-leg engaged in a furious altercation with someone overhead.

'Dog, I'll blow out your brains!' yelled a strange voice.

'Fire and smoke! blow out the candle first – ha, ha, ha! ho, ho, ho!' cried Wooden-leg; then there ensued the explosion of a pistol, a dreadful

G

stamping of feet, with the sound of several men swearing and fighting. To all this Ewen and his wife hearkened in fear and perplexity; at last something fell heavily on the floor, and then all became still, and not a sound was heard but the night wind sighing down the glen.

Betimes in the morning Ewen, weary and unslept, left his bed and ascended to the door of this terrible lodger and rapped gently.

'Come in; why the devil this fuss and ceremony, eh, comrade?' cried a hoarse voice, and there was old Wooden-leg, not lying dead on the floor as Ewen expected, or perhaps hoped; but stumping about in his shirt sleeves, pipe-claying his facings, and whistling the 'Point of War'.

On being questioned about the most unearthly 'row' of last night, he only bade Ewen mind his own affairs, or uttered a volley of oaths, some of which were Spanish, and mixing a can of gunpowder grog drained it at a draught.

He was very quarrelsome, dictatorial, and scandalously irreligious; thus his military reminiscences were of so ferocious and bloodthirsty a nature, that they were sufficient to scare any quiet man out of his seven senses. But it was more particularly in relating the butcheries, murders, and ravages of Cumberland in the highlands that he exulted, and there was always a terrible air of probability in all he said. On Ewen once asking of him if he had ever been punished for the many irregularities and cruelties he so freely acknowledged having committed,

'Punished? Fire and smoke, comrade, I should think so; I have been flogged till the bones of my back stood through the quivering flesh; I have been picquetted, tied neck and heels, or sent to ride the wooden horse, and to endure other punishments which are now abolished in the King's service. An officer once tied me neck and heels for eight and forty hours – ay, damme, till I lost my senses; but he lost his life soon after, a shot from the rear killed him; you understand me, comrade: ha, ha, ha! ho, ho, ho! a shot from the rear.'

'You murdered him?' said Ewen, in a tone of horror.

'I did not say so,' cried Wooden-leg with an oath, as he dealt his landlord a thwack across the shins with his stump; 'but I'll tell you how it happened. I was on the Carthagena expedition in '41, and served amid all the horrors of that bombardment, which was rendered unsuccessful by the quarrels of the general and admiral; then the yellow fever broke out among the troops, who were crammed on board the ships of war like figs in a cask, or like the cargo of a slaver, so they died in scores – and in scores their putrid corpses lay round the hawsers of the shipping, which raked them up every day as they swung round with the tide; and from all the open gunports, where their hammocks were hung, our sick men saw the ground sharks gorging themselves on the dead, while they daily expected to follow. The air was black with flies, and the scorching sun seemed to have leagued with the infernal Spaniards against us. But, fire and smoke, mix me some more grog, I am forgetting my story!

'Our Grenadiers, with those of other regiments, under Colonel James Grant of Carron, were landed on the Island of Tierrabomba, which lies at the entrance of the harbour of Carthagena, where we stormed two small forts which our ships had cannonaded on the previous day.

' "Grenadiers – open your pouches – handle grenades – blow your fuses!" cried Grant, "forward."

'And then we bayonetted the dons, or with the clubbed musket smashed their heads like ripe pumpkins, while our fleet, anchored with broadsides to the shore, threw shot and shell, grape, cannister, carcasses, and hand-grenades in showers among the batteries, booms, cables, chains, ships of war, gunboats, and the devil only knows what more.

'It was evening when we landed, and as the ramparts of San Luiz de Bocca Chica were within musket shot of our left flank, the lieutenant of our company was left with twelve grenadiers (of whom I was one) as a species of out-picquet to watch the Spaniards there, and to acquaint the officer in the captured forts if anything was essayed by way of sortie.

'About midnight I was posted as an advanced sentinel, and ordered to face La Bocca Chica with all my ears and eyes open. The night was close and sultry; there was not a breath of wind stirring on the land or waveless sea; and all was still save the cries of the wild animals that preyed upon the unburied dead, or the sullen splash caused by some half-shrouded corpse, as it was launched from a gun-port, for our ships were moored within pistol-shot of the place where I stood.

'Towards the west the sky was a deep and lurid red, as if the midnight sea was in flames at the horizon; and between me and this fiery glow, I could see the black and opaque outline of the masts, the yards, and the gigantic hulls of those floating charnel-houses our line-of-battle ships, and the dark solid ramparts of San Luiz de Bocca Chica.

'Suddenly I saw before me the head of a Spanish column!

'I cocked my musket, they seemed to be halted in close order, for I could see the white coats and black hats of a single company only. So I fired at them point blank, and fell back on the picquet, which stood to arms.

'The lieutenant of our grenadiers came hurrying towards me.

' "Where are the dons?" said he.

' "In our front, sir," said I, pointing to the white line which seemed to waver before us in the gloom under the walls of San Luiz, and then it disappeared.

' "They are advancing," said I.

' "They have vanished, fellow," said the lieutenant, angrily.

' "Because they have marched down into a hollow."

'In a moment after they reappeared, upon which the lieutenant brought up the picquet, and after firing three volleys retired towards the principal fort where Colonel Grant had all the troops under arms; but not a Spaniard approached us, and what, think you, deceived me and caused this alarm? Only a grove of trees, fire and smoke! yes, it was a grove of manchineel trees, which the Spaniards had cut down or burned to within five feet of the ground; and as their bark is white it resembled the Spanish uniform, while the black burned tops easily passed for their grenadier caps to the overstrained eyes of a poor anxious lad, who found himself under the heavy responsibility of an advanced sentinel for the first time in his life.'

'And was this the end of it?' asked Ewen.

'Hell and Tommy?' roared the Wooden-leg, 'no – but you shall hear. I was batooned by the lieutenant; then I was tried at the drumhead for causing a false alarm, and sentenced to be tied neck and heels, and lest you may not know the fashion of this punishment I shall tell you of it. I was placed on the ground; my firelock was put under my hams, and another was placed over my neck; then the two were drawn close together by two cartouch-box straps; and in this situation, doubled up as round as a ball, I remained with my chin wedged between my knees until the blood spouted out of my mouth, nose, and ears, and I became insensible. When I recovered my senses the troops were forming in column, preparatory to assaulting Fort San Lazare; and though almost blind, and both weak and trembling, I was forced to take my place in the ranks; and I ground my teeth as I handled my musket and saw the lieutenant of our company, in lace-ruffles and powdered wig, prepare to join the forlorn hope, which was composed of six hundred chosen grenadiers, under Colonel Grant, a brave

Scottish officer. I loaded my piece with a charmed bullet, cast in a mould given to me by an Indian warrior, and marched on with my section. The assault failed. Of the forlorn hope I alone escaped, for Grant and his Grenadiers perished to a man in the breach. There, too, lay our lieutenant. A shot had pierced his head behind, just at the queue. Queer, was it not? when I was his covering file?'

As he said this, Wooden-leg gave Ewen another of those diabolical leers, which always made his blood run cold, and continued,

'I passed him as he lay dead, with his sword in his hand, his fine ruffled shirt and silk waistcoat drenched with blood – by the bye, there was a pretty girl's miniature, with powdered hair peeping out of it too. "Ho, ho!" thought I, as I gave him a hearty kick; "you will never again have me tied neck-and-heels for not wearing spectacles on sentry, or get me a hundred lashes for not having my queue dressed straight to the seam of my coat".'

'Horrible!' said Ewen.

'I will wager my wooden leg against your two of flesh and bone, that your officer would have been served in the same way, if he had given you the same provocation.'

'Heaven forbid!' said Ewen.

'Ha, ha, ha! Ho, ho, ho!' cried Wooden-leg.

'You spoke of an Indian warrior,' said Ewen, uneasily, as the atrocious anecdotes of this hideous old man excited his anger and repugnance; 'then you have served, like myself, in the New World?'

'Fire and smoke! I should think so, but long before your day.'

'Then you fought against the Cherokees?'

'Yes.'

'At Warwomans Creek?'

'Yes; I was killed there.'

'You were – what?' stammered Ewen.

'Killed there.'

'Killed?'

'Yes, scalped by the Cherokees; dam! don't I speak plain enough?'

'He is mad,' thought Ewen.

'I am not mad,' said Wooden-leg gruffly.

'I never said so,' urged Ewen.

'Thunder and blazes! but you thought it, which is all the same.'

'I was killed there, and, moreover, buried too, by the Scots Royals, when they interred the dead next day.'

'Then how came you to be here?' said Ewen, not very much at ease, to find himself in company with one he deemed a lunatic.

'Here? that is my business – not yours,' was the surly rejoinder.

Ewen was silent, but reckoned over that now there were but thirty days to run until the 26th of April, when the stipulated year would expire.

'Yes, comrade, just thirty days,' said Wooden-leg, with an affirmative nod, divining the thoughts of Ewen; 'and then I shall be off, bag and baggage, if my friends come.'

'If not?'

'Then I shall remain where I am.'

'The Lord forbid!' thought Ewen; 'but I can apply to the sheriff.'

'Death and fury! Thunder and blazes! I should like to see the rascal of a sheriff who would dare to meddle with me!' growled the old fellow, as his one eye shot fire, and, limping away, he ascended the stairs grumbling and swearing, leaving poor Ewen terrified even to think, on finding that his thoughts, although only half conceived, were at once divined and responded to by this strange inmate of his house.

'His friends,' thought Ewen, 'who may they be?'

Three heavy knocks on the floor overhead, as a reply.

This queer old fellow was always in a state of great excitement, and used an extra number of oaths, and mixed his grog more thickly with gunpowder when a stray red coat appeared far down the long green glen, which was crossed by Ewen's lonely toll-bar. Then he would get into a prodigious fuss and bustle, and was wont to pack and cord his trunk, to brush up his well-worn and antique regimentals, and to adjust his queue and the black cockade of his triple-cornered hat, as if preparing to depart.

As the time of that person's wished-for departure drew nigh, Ewen took courage, and shaking off the timidity with which the swearing and boisterous fury of Wooden-leg had impressed him, he ventured to expostulate a little on the folly and sin of his unmeaning oaths, and the atrocity of the crimes he boasted of having committed.

But the wicked old Wooden-leg laughed and swore more than ever, saying that a 'true soldier was never a religious one'.

'You are wrong, comrade,' retorted the old Cameronian, taking fire at such an assertion; 'religion is the lightest burden a poor soldier can carry;

and, moreover, it hath upheld me on many a long day's march, when almost sinking under hunger and fatigue, with my pack, kettle, and sixty rounds of ball ammunition on my back. The duties of a good and brave soldier are no way incompatible with those of a Christian man; and I never lay down to rest on the wet bivouac or bloody field, with my knapsack, or it might be a dead comrade, for a pillow, without thanking God –'

'Ha, ha, ha!'

'– The God of Scotland's covenanted Kirk for the mercies he vouchsafed to Ewen Mac Ewen, a poor grenadier of the 26th Regiment.'

'Ho, ho, ho!'

The old Cameronian took off his bonnet and lifted up his eyes, as he spoke fervently, and with the simple reverence of the olden time; but Wooden-leg grinned and chuckled and gnashed his teeth as Ewen resumed.

'A brave soldier may rush to the cannon's mouth, though it be loaded with grape and cannister; or at a line of levelled bayonets – and rush fearlessly too – and yet he may tremble, without shame, at the thought of Hell, or of offended Heaven. Is it not so, comrade? I shall never forget the words of our chaplain before we stormed the Isle of Saba and St Martin from the Dutch, with Admiral Rodney, in '81.'

'Bah – that was after I was killed by the Cherokees. Well?'

'The Cameronians were formed in line, mid leg in the salt water, with bayonets fixed, the colours flying, the pipes playing and drums beating "Britons strike home", and our chaplain, a reverend minister of God's word, stood beside the colonel with the shot and shell from the Dutch batteries flying about his old white head, but he was cool and calm, for he was the grandson of Richard Cameron, the glorious martyr of Airdsmoss.

' "Fear not, my bairns," cried he (he aye called us his bairns, having ministered unto us for fifty years and more) – "fear not; but remember that the eyes of the Lord are on every righteous soldier, and that His hand will shield him in the day of battle!"

' "Forward, my lads," cried the colonel, waving his broad sword, while the musket shot shaved the curls of his old brigadier wig; "forward, and at them with your bayonets;" and bravely we fell on – eight hundred Scotsmen, shoulder to shoulder – and in half an hour the British flag was waving over the Dutchman's Jack on the ramparts of St Martin.'

But to all Ewen's exordiums, the Wooden-leg replied by oaths, or mockery, or his incessant laugh,

'Ha, ha, ha! Ho, ho, ho!'

At last came the long-wished for twenty-sixth of April!

The day was dark and louring. The pine woods looked black, and the slopes of the distant hills seemed close and near, and yet gloomy withal. The sky was veiled by masses of hurrying clouds, which seemed to chase each other across the Moray Firth. That estuary was flecked with foam, and the ships were riding close under the lee of the Highland shore, with topmasts struck, their boats secured, and both anchors out, for everything betokened a coming storm.

And with night it came in all its fury; – a storm similar to that of the preceding year.

The fierce and howling wind swept through the mountain gorges, and levelled the lonely shielings, whirling their fragile roofs into the air, and uprooting strong pines and sturdy beeches; the water was swept up from the Lock of the Clans, and mingled with the rain which drenched the woods around it. The green and yellow lightning played in ghastly gleams about the black summit of Dun Daviot, and again the rolling thunder bellowed over the graves of the dead on the bleak, dark moor of Culloden. Attracted by the light in the windows of the toll house, the red deer came down from the hills in herds and cowered near the little dwelling; while the cries of the affrighted partridges, blackcocks, and even those of the gannets from the Moray Firth were heard at times, as they were swept past, with branches, leaves, and stones, on the skirts of the hurrying blast.

'It is just such a storm as we had this night twelve months ago,' said Meinie, whose cheek grew pale at the elemental uproar.

'There will be no one coming up the glen tonight,' replied Ewen; 'so I may as well secure the toll-bar, lest a gust should dash it to pieces.'

It required no little skill or strength to achieve this in such a tempest; the gate was strong and heavy, but it was fastened at last, and Ewen retreated to his own fireside. Meanwhile, during all this frightful storm without, Wooden-leg was heard singing and carolling upstairs, stumping about in the lulls of the tempest, and rolling, pushing, and tumbling his chest from side to side; then he descended to get a fresh can of grog – for 'grog, grog, grog,' was ever his cry. His old withered face was flushed, and his excited eye shone like a baleful star. He was conscious that a great event would ensue.

Ewen felt happy in his soul that his humble home should no longer be the resting-place of this evil bird whom the last tempest had blown hither.

'So you leave us tomorrow, comrade?' said he.

'I'll march before daybreak,' growled the other; "twas our old fashion in the days of Minden. Huske and Hawley always marched off in the dark.'

'Before daybreak?'

'Fire and smoke, I have said so, and you shall see; for my friends are on the march already; but good night, for I shall have to parade betimes. They come; though far, far off as yet.'

He retired with one of his diabolical leers, and Ewen and his wife ensconced themselves in the recesses of their warm box-bed; Meinie soon fell into a sound sleep, though the wind continued to howl, the rain to lash against the trembling walls of the little mansion, and the thunder to hurl peal after peal across the sky of that dark and tempestuous night.

The din of the elements and his own thoughts kept Ewen long awake; but though the gleams of electric light came frequent as ever through the little window, the glow of the 'gathering peat' sank lower on the hearth of hard-beaten clay, and the dull measured tick-tack of the drowsy clock as it fell on the drum of his ear, about midnight, was sending him to sleep, by the weariness of its intense monotony, when from a dream that the fierce hawk eye of his malevolent lodger was fixed upon him, he started suddenly to full consciousness. An uproar of tongues now rose and fell upon the gusts of wind without; and he heard an authoritative voice requiring the toll-bar to be opened.

Overhead rang the stumping of the Wooden-leg, whose hoarse voice was heard bellowing in reply from the upper window.

'The Lord have a care of us!' muttered Mac Ewen, as he threw his kilt and plaid round him, thrust on his bonnet and brogues, and hastened to the door, which was almost blown in by the tempest as he opened it.

The night was as dark, and the hurricane as furious as ever; but how great was Ewen's surprise to see the advanced guard of a corps of Grenadiers, halted at the toll-bar gate, which he hastened to unlock, and the moment he did so, it was torn off its iron hooks and swept up the glen like a leaf from a book, or a lady's handkerchief; as with an unearthly howling the wind came tearing along in fitful and tremendous gusts, which made the strongest forests stoop, and dashed the struggling coasters on the rocks of the Firth – the *Æstuarium Vararis* of the olden time.

As the levin brands burst in lurid fury overhead, they seemed to strike fire from the drenched rocks, the dripping trees, and the long line of flooded roadway, that wound through the pastoral glen towards Culloden.

The advanced guard marched on in silence with arms slung; and Ewen, to prevent himself from being swept away by the wind, clung with both hands to a stone pillar of the bar gate, that he might behold the passage of this midnight regiment, which approached in firm and silent order in sections of twelve files abreast, all with muskets slung. The pioneers were in front, with their leather aprons, axes, saws, bill-hooks, and hammers; the band was at the head of the column; the drums, fifes, and colours were in the centre; the captains were at the head of their companies; the subalterns on the reverse flank, and the field-officers were all mounted on black chargers, that curvetted and pranced like shadows, without a sound.

Slowly they marched, but erect and upright, not a man of them seeming to stoop against the wind or rain, while overhead the flashes of the broad and blinding lightning were blazing like a ghastly torch, and making every musket-barrel, every belt-plate, sword-blade, and buckle, gleam as this mysterious corpse filed through the barrier, with who? Wooden-leg among them!

By the incessant gleams Ewen could perceive that they were Grenadiers, and wore the quaint old uniform of George II's time; the sugar-loaf-shaped cap of red cloth embroidered with worsted; the great square-tailed red coat with its heavy cuffs and close-cut collar; the stockings rolled above the knee, and enormous shoe-buckles. They carried grenadopouches; the officers had espontoons; the sergeants shouldered heavy halberds, and the coats of the little drum-boys were covered with fantastic lace.

It was not the quaint and antique aspect of this solemn battalion that terrified Ewen, or chilled his heart; but the ghastly expression of their faces, which were pale and hollow-eyed, being, to all appearance, the visages of spectres; and they marched past like a long and wavering panorama, without a sound; for though the wind was loud, and the rain was drenching, neither could have concealed the measured tread of so many mortal feet; but there was no footfall heard on the roadway, nor the tramp of a charger's hoof; the regiment defiled past, noiseless as a wreath of smoke.

The pallor of their faces, and the stillness which accompanied their march, were out of the course of nature; and the soul of Mac Ewen died away within him; but his eyes were riveted upon the marching phantoms –

if phantoms, indeed, they were – as if by fascination; and, like one in a terrible dream, he continued to gaze until the last files were past; and with them rode a fat and full-faced officer, wearing a three-cocked hat, and having a star and blue ribbon on his breast. His face ghastly like the rest, and dreadfully distorted, as if by mental agony and remorse. Two aides-de-camp accompanied him, and he rode a wild-looking black horse, whose eyes shot fire. At the neck of the fat spectre – for a spectre he really seemed – hung a card.

It was the Nine of Diamonds!

The whole of this silent and mysterious battalion passed in line of march up the glen, with the gleams of lightning flashing about them. One bolt more brilliant than the rest brought back the sudden flash of steel.

They had fixed bayonets, and shouldered arms!

And on and on they marched, diminishing in the darkness and the distance, those ghastly Grenadiers, towards the flat bleak moor of Culloden, with the green lightning playing about them, and gleaming on the storm-swept waste.

The Wooden-leg – Ewen's unco' guest – disappeared with them, and was never heard of more in Strathnairn.

He had come with a tempest, and gone with one. Neither was any trace ever seen or heard of those strange and silent soldiers. No regiment had left Nairn that night, and no regiment reached Inverness in the morning; so unto this day the whole affair remains a mystery, and a subject for ridicule with some, although Ewen – whose story of the midnight march of a corpse in time of war caused his examination by the authorities in the Castle of Inverness – stuck manfully to his assertions, which were further corroborated by the evidence of his wife and children. He made a solemn affidavit of the circumstances I have related before the sheriff, whose court books will be found to confirm them in every particular; if not, it is the aforesaid sheriff's fault, and not mine.

There were not a few (but these were generally old Jacobite ladies of decayed Highland families, who form the gossiping tabbies and wall-flowers of the Northern Meeting) who asserted that in their young days they had heard of such a regiment marching by night, once a year to the field of Culloden; for it is currently believed by the most learned on such subjects in the vicinity of the 'Clach na Cudden', that on the anniversary of the sorrowful battle, a *certain place*, which shall be nameless, opens, and that the restless souls of the murderers of the wounded clansmen march in military array to the green graves upon the purple heath, in yearly penance; and this story was thought to receive full corroboration by the apparition of a fat lubberly spectre with the nine of diamonds chained to his neck; as it was on that card – since named the Curse of Scotland – the Duke of Cumberland hastily pencilled the savage order to 'show no quarter to the wounded, but to slaughter all'.

CAPTAIN GEORGE ELIOT

Montgomery of Alamein briefly described the military activity in the East during the nineteenth century in the following way. 'British forces in India were constantly occupied and in 1837, with the First Afghan War, a new phase of war and conquest began which lasted for twenty years. The north-west frontier had to be secured; Sind was brought under control in 1843 . . . and the Sikhs were defeated at Gujarat in 1849. The British position in India was then imperilled by the mutiny of the native army of the East India Company in 1857–8. . . . The British also took the lead in the general competition of the European powers to exploit China, where the Opium War took place between 1839 and 1842, and the Taiping rebellion between 1850 and 1864. While the British and French preyed on China in the south and east, the Russians grabbed what they could in the north and west.'

Captain George Eliot of the US Army has written a tale in which the atmosphere of horror stems not from the supernatural but from the time in which it was set. When printed in the Xmas 1928 issue of *Weird Tales* it was named the best story of the month by its readers and in recent years Reginald Smith wrote, in a study of horror stories, '*The Copper Bowl* is undoubtedly the most effectively gruesome and sickening horror tale to appear during the entire history of *Weird Tales*, or anywhere else for that matter.' In it the capture of a French officer by the Chinese leads to a horrifying situation.

7 · THE COPPER BOWL

Yuan Li, the mandarin, leaned back in his rosewood chair.

'It is written,' he said softly, 'that a good servant is a gift of the gods, whilst a bad one –'

The tall, powerfully built man standing humbly before the robed figure in the chair bowed thrice, hastily, submissively.

Fear glinted in his eye, though he was armed, and moreover was accounted a brave soldier. He could have broken the little smooth-faced mandarin across his knee, and yet –

'Ten thousand pardons, beneficent one,' he said. 'I have done all – having regard to your honourable order to slay the man not nor do him permanent injury – I have done all that I can. But –'

'But he speaks not!' murmured the mandarin. 'And you come to me with a tale of failure? I do not like failures, Captain Wang!'

The mandarin toyed with a little paper-knife on the low table beside him. Wang shuddered.

'Well, no matter for this one time,' the mandarin said after a moment. Wang breathed a sigh of most heartfelt relief, and the mandarin smiled softly, fleetingly. 'Still,' he went on, 'our task is yet to be accomplished. We have the man – he has the information we require; surely some way may be found. The servant has failed; now the master must try his hand. Bring the man to me.'

Wang bowed low and departed with considerable haste.

The mandarin sat silent for a moment, looking across the wide, sunlit room at a pair of singing birds in a wicker cage hanging in the farther window. Presently he nodded – one short, satisfied nod – and struck a little silver bell which stood on his beautifully inlaid table.

Instantly, a white-robed, silent-footed servant entered, and stood with bowed head awaiting his master's pleasure. To him Yuan Li gave certain swift, incisive orders.

The white-robed one had scarcely departed when Wang, captain of the mandarin's guard, re-entered the spacious apartment.

'The prisoner, Benevolent!' he announced.

The mandarin made a slight motion with his slender hand; Wang barked an order, and there entered, between two heavily-muscled, half-naked guardsmen, a short, sturdily built man, barefooted, clad only in a tattered shirt and khaki trousers, but with fearless blue eyes looking straight at Yuan Li under the tousled masses of his blond hair.

A white man!

'Ah!' said Yuan Li, in his calm way, speaking faultless French. 'The excellent Lieutenant Fournet! Still obstinate?'

Fournet cursed him earnestly, in French and three different Chinese dialects.

'You'll pay for this, Yuan Li!' he wound up. 'Don't think your filthy brutes can try the knuckle-torture and their other devil's tricks on a French officer and get away with it!'

Yuan Li toyed with his paper-knife, smiling.

'You threaten me, Lieutenant Fournet,' he answered, 'yet your threats are but as rose-petals wafted away on the morning breeze – unless you return to your post to make your report.'

'Why, damn you!' answered the prisoner. 'You needn't try that sort of thing – you know better than to kill me! My commandant is perfectly aware of my movements – he'll be knocking on your door with a company of the Legion at his back if I don't show up by tomorrow at reveille!'

Yuan Li smiled again.

'Doubtless – and yet we still have the better part of the day before us,' he said. 'Much may be accomplished in an afternoon and evening.'

Fournet swore again.

'You can torture me and be damned,' he answered. 'I know and you know that you don't dare to kill me or to injure me so that I can't get back to Fort Deschamps. For the rest, do your worst, you yellow-skinned brute!'

'A challenge!' the mandarin exclaimed. 'And I will indeed pick up your glove! Look, Lieutenant, what I require from you is the strength and location of your outpost on the Mephong River. So –'

'So that your cursed bandits, whose murders and lootings keep you here in luxury, can rush the outpost some dark night and open the river route for their boats,' Fournet cut in. 'I know you, Yuan Li, and I know your trade – mandarin of thieves! The military governor of Tonkin sent a battalion of the Foreign Legion here to deal with such as you, and to restore peace and order on the frontier, not to yield to childish threats! That is not the Legion's way, and you should know it. The best thing you can do is to send in your submission, or I can assure you that within a fortnight your head will be rotting over the North Gate of Hanoi, as a warning to others who might follow your bad example.'

The mandarin's smile never altered, though well he knew that this was no idle threat. With Tonkinese tirailleurs, even with Colonial infantry, he could make some sort of headway, but these thrice-accursed Legionnaires were devils from the very pit itself. He – Yuan Li, who had ruled as king in the valley of the Mephong, to whom half a Chinese province and many a square mile of French Tonkin had paid tribute humbly – felt his throne of power tottering beneath him. But one hope remained; down the river, beyond the French outposts, were boats filled with men and with the loot of a dozen villages – the most successful raiding-party he had ever sent out. Let these boats come through, let him have back his men (and they were his best), get his hands on the loot, and perhaps something might be done. Gold, jewels, jade – and though the soldiers of France were terrible,

H

there were in Hanoi certain civilian officials not wholly indifferent to these things. But on the banks of Mephong, as though they knew his hopes, the Foreign Legion had established an outpost – he must know exactly where, he must know exactly how strong; for till this river post was gone, the boats could never reach him.

And now Lieutenant Fournet, staff officer to the commandant, had fallen into his hands. All night his torturers had reasoned with the stubborn young soldier, and all morning they had never left him for a minute. They had marked him in no way, nor broken bones, nor so much as cut or bruised the skin – yet there are ways! Fournet shuddered all over at the thought of what he had gone through, that age-long night and morning.

To Fournet, his duty came first: to Yuan Li, it was life or death that Fournet should speak. And he had taken measures which now marched to their fulfilment.

He dared not go to extremes with Fournet; not yet could French justice connect the Mandarin Yuan Li with the bandits of the Mephong.

They were suspect, but they could not prove; and an outrage such as the killing or maiming of a French officer in his own palace was more than Yuan Li dared allow. He walked on thin ice indeed those summer days, and walked warily.

Yet – he had taken measures.

'My head is still securely on my shoulders,' he replied to Fournet. 'I do not think it will decorate your gate-spikes. So you will not speak?'

'Certainly not!'

Lieutenant Fournet's words were as firm as his jaw.

'Ah, but you will. Wang!'

'Magnanimous!'

'Four more guards. Make the prisoner secure.'

Wang clapped his hands.

Instantly four additional half-naked men sprang into the room; two, falling on their knees, seized Fournet round the legs; another threw his corded arms round the lieutenant's waist; another stood by, club in hand, as a reserve in case of – what?

The two original guards still retained their grip on Fournet's arms.

Now, in the grip of those sinewy hands, he was held immovable, utterly helpless, a living statue.

Yuan Li, the mandarin, smiled again. One who did not know him would have thought his smile held an infinite tenderness, a divine compassion.

He touched the bell at his side.

Instantly, in the farther doorway, appeared two servants, conducting a veiled figure – a woman, shrouded in a dark drapery.

A word from Yuan Li – rough hands tore the veil aside, and there stood drooping between the impassive servants a vision of loveliness, a girl scarce out of her teens, dark-haired, slender, with the great appealing brown eyes of a fawn: eyes which widened suddenly as they rested on Lieutenant Fournet.

'Lily!' exclaimed Fournet, and his five guards had their hands full to hold him as he struggled to be free.

'You fiend!' he spat at Yuan Li. 'If a hair of this girl's head is touched, by the Holy Virgin of Yvetot I will roast you alive in the flames of your own palace! My God, Lily, how –'

'Quite simply, my dear lieutenant,' the mandarin's silky voice interrupted. 'We knew, of course – every house-servant in North Tonkin is a spy of mine – that you had conceived an affection for this woman; and when I heard you were proving obdurate under the little attentions of my men, I thought it well to send for her. Her father's bungalow is far from the post – indeed, it is in Chinese and not French territory, as you know – and the task was not a difficult one. And now –'

'André! André!' the girl was crying, struggling in her turn with the servants. 'Save me, André – these beasts –'

'Have no fear, Lily,' André Fournet replied. 'They dare not harm you, any more than they dare to kill me. They are bluffing –'

'But have you considered well, lieutenant?' asked the mandarin gently. 'You, of course, are a French officer. The arm of France – and it is a long and unforgiving arm – will be stretched out to seize your murderers. The gods forbid I should set that arm reaching for me and mine. But this girl – ah, that is different!'

'Different? How is it different? The girl is a French citizen –'

'I think not, my good Lieutenant Fournet. She is three-quarters French in blood, true; but her father is half Chinese, and is a Chinese subject; she is a resident of China – I think you will find that French justice will not be prepared to avenge her death quite so readily as your own. At any rate, it is a chance I am prepared to take.'

Fournet's blood seemed to turn to ice in his veins. The smiling devil was right! Lily – his lovely white Lily, whose only mark of Oriental blood was the rather piquant slant of her great eyes – was not entitled to the protection of the tricolour.

God! What a position! Either betray his flag, his regiment, betray his comrades to their deaths – or see his Lily butchered before his eyes!

'So now, Lieutenant Fournet, we understand each other,' Yuan Li continued after a brief pause to let the full horror of the situation grip the other's soul. 'I think you will be able to remember the location and strength of that outpost for me – now?'

Fournet stared at the man in bitter silence, but the words had given the quick-minded Lily a key to the situation, which she had hardly understood at first.

'No, no, André!' she cried. 'Do not tell him. Better that I should die than you should be a traitor! See – I am ready.'

Fournet threw back his head: his wavering resolution reincarnate.

'The girl shames me!' he said. 'Slay her if you must, Yuan Li – and if France will not avenge her, *I will*! But traitor I will not be!'

'I do not think that is your last word, lieutenant,' the mandarin purred. 'Were I to strangle the girl, yes – perhaps. But first she must cry to you for help, and when you hear her screaming in agony, the woman you love, perhaps then you will forget these noble heroics!'

Again he clapped his hands; and again silent servants glided into the room. One bore a small brazier of glowing charcoal; a second a little cage of thick wire mesh, inside of which something moved horribly; a third bore a copper bowl with handles on each side, to which was attached a steel band that glittered in the sunlight.

The hair rose on the back of Fournet's neck. What horror impended now? Deep within him some instinct warned him that what was now to follow would be fiendish beyond the mind of mortal man to conceive. The mandarin's eyes seemed suddenly to glow with infernal fires. Was he in truth man – or demon?

A sharp word in some Yunnan dialect unknown to Fournet – and the servants had flung the girl upon her back on the floor, spread-eagled in pitiful helplessness, upon a magnificent peacock rug.

Another word from the mandarin's thin lips – and roughly they tore the clothing from the upper half of the girl's body. White and silent she lay upon that splendid rug, her eyes still on Fournet's: silent, lest words of hers should impair the resolution of the man she loved.

Fournet struggled furiously with his guards: but they were five strong men, and they held him fast.

'Remember, Yuan Li!' he panted. 'You'll pay! – damn your yellow soul –'

The mandarin ignored the threat.

'Proceed,' he said to the servants. 'Note carefully, Monsieur le Lieutenant Fournet, what we are doing. First, you will note, the girl's wrists and ankles are lashed to posts and to heavy articles of furniture, suitably placed so that she cannot move. You wonder at the strength of the rope, the number of turns we take to hold so frail a girl? I assure you, they will be required. Under the copper bowl, I have seen a feeble old man tear his wrist free from an iron chain.'

The mandarin paused; the girl was now bound so tightly that she could scarce move a muscle of her body.

Yuan Li regarded the arrangements.

'Well done,' he approved. 'Yet if she tears any limb free, the man who bound that limb shall have an hour under the bamboo rods. Now – the bowl! Let me see it.'

He held out a slender hand. Respectfully a servant handed him the bowl, with its dangling band of flexible steel. Fournet, watching with eyes full of dread, saw that the band was fitted with a lock, adjustable to various positions. It was like a belt, a girdle.

'Very well,' the mandarin nodded, turning the thing over and over in fingers that almost seemed to caress it. 'But I anticipate – perhaps the lieutenant and the young lady are not familiar with this little device. Let me explain, or rather, demonstrate. Put the bowl in place, Kan-su. No, no – just the bowl, this time.'

Another servant, who had started forward, stepped back into his corner. The man addressed as Kan-su took the bowl, knelt at the side of the girl, passed the steel band under her body and placed the bowl, bottom up, on her naked abdomen, tugging at the girdle till the rim of the bowl bit into the soft flesh. Then he snapped the lock fast, holding the bowl thus firmly in place by the locked steel belt attached to its two handles and passing round the girl's waist. He rose, stood silent with folded arms.

Fournet felt his flesh crawling with horror – and all this time Lily had said not one word, though the tight girdle, the pressure of the circular rim of the bowl, must have been hurting her cruelly.

But now she spoke, bravely.

'Do not give away, André,' she said. 'I can bear it – it does – it does not hurt!'

'God!' yelled André Fournet, still fighting vainly against those clutching yellow hands.

'It does not hurt!' the mandarin echoed the girl's last words.

'Well, perhaps not. But we will take it off, notwithstanding. We must be merciful.'

At his order the servant removed bowl and girdle. An angry red circle showed on the white skin of the girl's abdomen where the rim had rested.

'And still I do not think you understand, *Mademoiselle* and *Monsieur*,' he went on. 'For presently we must apply the bowl again – and when we do, under it we will put – *this*!'

With a swift movement of his arm he snatched from the servant in the corner the wire cage and held it up to the sunlight.

The eyes of Fournet and Lily fixed themselves upon it in horror. For within, plainly seen now, moved a great grey rat – a whiskered, beady-eyed, restless, scabrous rat, its white chisel-teeth shining through the mesh.

'Dieu de Dieu!' breathed Fournet. His mind refused utterly to grasp the full import of the dreadful fate that was to be Lily's; he could only stare at the unquiet rat – stare – stare –

'You understand *now*, I am sure,' purred the mandarin. 'The rat under the bowl – observe the bottom of the bowl, note the little flange. Here we put the hot charcoal – the copper becomes heated – the heat is overpowering – the rat cannot support it – he has but one means of escape: he gnaws his way out through the lady's body! And now about that outpost, Lieutenant Fournet?'

'No – no – *no*!' cried Lily. 'They will not do it – they are trying to frighten us – they are human; men cannot do a thing like that – be silent, André, be silent, whatever happens; don't let them beat you! Don't let them make a traitor of you! Ah –'

At a wave from the mandarin, the servant with the bowl again approached the half-naked girl. But this time the man with the cage stepped forward also. Deftly he thrust in a hand, avoided the rat's teeth, jerked the struggling vermin out by the scruff of the neck.

The bowl was placed in position. Fournet fought desperately for freedom – if only he could get one arm clear, snatch a weapon of some sort!

Lily gave a sudden little choking cry.

The rat had been thrust under the bowl.

Click! the steel girdle was made fast – and now they were piling the red-hot charcoal on the upturned bottom of the bowl, while Lily writhed in her bonds as she felt the wriggling, pattering horror of the rat on her bare skin, under that bowl of fiends.

One of the servants handed a tiny object to the impassive mandarin.

Yuan Li held it up in one hand.

It was a little key.

'This key, Lieutenant Fournet,' he said, 'unlocks the steel girdle which holds the bowl in place. It is yours – as a reward for the information I require. Will you not be reasonable? Soon it will be too late!'

Fournet looked at Lily. The girl was quiet, now, had ceased to struggle; her eyes were open, or he would have thought she had fainted.

The charcoal glowed redly on the bottom of the copper bowl. And beneath its carven surface, Fournet could imagine the great grey rat stirring restlessly, turning around and around, seeking escape from the growing heat, at last sinking his teeth in that soft white skin, gnawing, burrowing, desperately.

God!

His duty – his flag – his regiment – France! Young Sous-lieutenant Pierre Desjardins – gay young Pierre, and twenty men – to be surprised and massacred, horribly, some saved for the torture, by an overwhelming rush of bandit-devils, through his treachery? He knew in his heart that he could not do it.

He must be strong – he must be firm.

If only he might suffer for Lily – gentle, loving little Lily, brave little Lily who had never harmed a soul.

Loud and clear through the room rang a terrible scream.

André, turning in fascinated horror, saw that Lily's body, straining upwards in an arc from the rug, was all but tearing asunder the bonds which held it. He saw, what he had not before noticed, that a little nick had been broken from one edge of the bowl – and through the nick and across the white surface of the girl's heaving body was running a tiny trickle of blood!

The rat was at work.

Then something snapped in André's brain. He went mad.

With the strength that is given to madmen, he tore loose his right arm from the grip that held it – tore loose, and dashed his fist into the face of the guard. The man with the club sprang forward unwarily; the next moment André had the weapon, and was laying about him with berserk fury. Three guards were down before Wang drew his sword and leaped into the fray.

Wang was a capable and well-trained soldier. It was cut, thrust and parry for a moment, steel against wood – then Wang, borne back before that terrible rush, had the reward of his strategy.

The two remaining guards, to whom he had signalled, and a couple of the servants flung themselves together on Fournet's back and bore him roaring to the floor.

The girl screamed again, shattering the coarser sounds of battle.

Fournet heard her – even in his madness he heard her. And as he heard, a knife hilt in a servant's girdle met his hand. He caught at it, thrust upward savagely; a man howled; the weight on Fournet's back grew less; blood gushed over his neck and shoulders. He thrust again, rolled clear of the press, and saw one man sobbing out his life from a ripped-open throat, while another, with both hands clasped over his groin, writhed in silent agony upon the floor.

André Fournet, gathering a knee under him, sprang like a panther straight at the throat of Wang the captain.

Down the two men went, rolling over and over on the floor. Wang's weapons clashed and clattered – a knife rose, dripping blood, and plunged home.

With a shout of triumph André Fournet sprang to his feet, his terrible knife in one hand, Wang's sword in the other.

Screaming, the remaining servants fled before that awful figure.

Alone, Yuan Li the mandarin faced incarnate vengeance.

'The key!'

Hoarsely Fournet spat out his demand; his reeling brain had room for but one thought:

'The key, you yellow demon!'

Yuan Li took a step backwards into the embrasured window, through which the jasmine-scented afternoon breeze still floated sweetly.

The palace was built on the edge of a cliff; below that window-ledge, the precipice fell sheer fifty feet down to the rocks and shallows of the upper Mephong.

Yuan Li smiled once more, his calm unruffled.

'You have beaten me, Fournet,' he said, 'yet I have beaten you too. I wish you joy of your victory. Here is the key.' He held it up in his hand; and as André sprang forward with a shout, Yuan Li turned, took one step to the window-ledge, and without another word was gone into space, taking the key with him.

Far below he crashed in red horror on the rocks, and the waters of the turbulent Mephong closed for ever over the key to the copper bowl.

Back sprang André – back to Lily's side. The blood ran no more from under the edge of the bowl; Lily lay very still, very cold.

God! She was dead!

Her heart was silent in her tortured breast.

André tore vainly at the bowl, the steel girdle – tore with bleeding fingers, with broken teeth, madly – in vain.

He could not move them.

And Lily was dead.

Or was she? What was that?

In her side a pulse beat – beat strongly and more strongly.

Was there still hope?

The mad Fournet began chafing her body and arms.

Could he revive her? Surely she was not dead – could not be dead!

The pulse still beat – strange it beat only in one place, on her soft white side, down under her last rib –

He kissed her cold and unresponsive lips.

When he raised his head the pulse had ceased to beat. Where it had been, blood was flowing sluggishly – dark venous blood, flowing in purple horror.

And from the midst of it, out of the girl's side, the grey, pointed head of the rat was thrust, its muzzle dripping gore, its black eyes glittering beadily at the madman who gibbered and frothed above it.

So, an hour later, his comrades found André Fournet and Lily his beloved – the tortured maniac keening over the tortured dead.

But the grey rat they never found.

ARTHUR MACHEN

This collection could not be considered complete without a contribution from the author who made supernatural stories of military men his own particular field. Arthur Machen (1863–1947) wrote many weird stories, but most famous of all was *The Bowman* which first appeared in the London *Evening News* in September, 1914, and upon which was founded the legend of the 'Angels of Mons' which captured the imagination of thousands. It told of British soldiers who were assisted in battle by gigantic, ghostly bowmen reminiscent of those who won the Battle of Agincourt. Immediately reports were received from the front that soldiers had actually seen these bowmen and that the bodies of German soldiers were often found with arrow-wounds. Numerous articles were written to affirm the reality of such reports.

Machen tried to convince people that his story was fiction but nobody listened and the legend grew from strength to strength and it is still remembered, truth often being attributed to it, over sixty years later. He also asserted, after the First World War, that *The Bowman* was a revised version of an earlier story *The Soldiers' Rest* and it is because it was the original basis of the 'Angels of Mons' legend that this story is included in this collection.

8 · THE SOLDIERS' REST

THE soldier with the ugly wound in the head opened his eyes at last, and looked about him with an air of pleasant satisfaction.

He still felt drowsy and dazed with some fierce experience through which he had passed, but so far he could not recollect much about it. But an agreeable glow began to steal about his heart – such a glow as comes to people who have been in a tight place and have come through it better than they had expected. In its mildest form this set of emotions may be observed in passengers who have crossed the Channel on a windy day without being sick. They triumph a little internally, and are suffused with vague, kindly feelings.

The wounded soldier was somewhat of this disposition as he opened his eyes, pulled himself together, and looked about him. He felt a sense of delicious ease and repose in bones that had been racked and weary, and deep in the heart that had so lately been tormented there was an assurance of comfort – of the battle won. The thundering, roaring waves were passed; he had entered into the haven of calm waters. After fatigues and terrors that as yet he could not recollect he seemed now to be resting in the easiest of all chairs in a dim, low room.

In the hearth there was a glint of fire and a blue, sweet-scented puff of wood smoke; a great black oak beam roughly hewn crossed the ceiling. Through the leaded panes of the windows he saw a rich glow of sunlight, green lawns, and against the deepest and most radiant of all blue skies the wonderful far-lifted towers of a vast Gothic cathedral – mystic, rich with imagery.

'Good Lord!' he murmured to himself. 'I didn't know they had such places in France. It's just like Wells. And it might be the other day when I was going past the Swan, just as it might be past that window, and asked the ostler what time it was, and he says, "What time? Why, summertime"; and there outside it looks like summer that would last for ever. If this was an inn they ought to call it "The Soldiers' Rest".'

He dozed off again, and when he opened his eyes once more a kindly looking man in some sort of black robe was standing by him.

'It's all right now, isn't it?' he said, speaking in good English.

'Yes, thank you, sir, as right as can be. I hope to be back again soon.'

'Well, well; but how did you come here? Where did you get that?' He pointed to the wound on the soldier's forehead.

The soldier put his hand up to his brow and looked dazed and puzzled.

'Well, sir,' he said at last, 'it was like this, to begin at the beginning. You know how we came over in August, and there we were in the thick of it, as you might say, in a day or two. An awful time it was, and I don't know how I got through it alive. My best friend was killed dead beside me as we lay in the trenches. By Cambrai, I think it was.

'Then things got a little quieter for a bit, and I was quartered in a village for the best part of a week. She was a very nice lady where I was, and she treated me proper with the best of everything. Her husband he was fighting; but she had the nicest little boy I ever knew, a little fellow of five or six it might be, and we got on splendid. The amount of their lingo that kid taught me – "We, we" and "Bong swor" and "Commong voo porty voo", and all – and I taught him English. You should have heard that nipper say "Arf a mo', old un"! It was a treat.

'Then one day we got surprised. There was about a dozen of us in the village, and two or three hundred Germans came down on us early one morning. They got us; no help for it. Before we could shoot.

'Well, there we were. They tied our hands behind our backs, and smacked our faces and kicked us a bit, and we were lined up opposite the house where I'd been staying.

'And then that poor little chap broke away from his mother, and he run out and saw one of the Boshes, as we call them, fetch me one over the jaw with his clenched fist. Oh dear! oh dear! he might have done it a dozen times if only that little child hadn't seen him.

'He had a poor bit of a toy I'd bought him at the village shop; a toy gun it was. And out he came running, as I say, crying out something in French like "Bad man! bad man! don't hurt my Anglish or I shoot you"; and he pointed that gun at the German soldier. The German, he took his bayonet, and he drove it right through the poor little chap's throat.'

The soldier's face worked and twitched and twisted itself into a sort of grin, and he sat grinding his teeth and staring at the man in the black robe. He was silent for a little. And then he found his voice, and the oaths rolled terrible, thundering from him, as he cursed that murderous wretch, and

bade him go down and burn for ever in hell. And the tears were raining down his face, and they choked him at last.

'I beg your pardon, sir, I'm sure,' he said, 'especially you being a minister of some kind. I suppose; but I can't help it. He was such a dear little man.'

The man in black murmured something to himself: *'Pretiosa in conspectu Domini mors innocentium ejus'* – Dear in the sight of the Lord is the death of His innocents. Then he put a kind hand very gently on the soldier's shoulder.

'Never mind,' said he; 'I've seen some service in my time, myself. But what about the wound?'

'Oh, that; that's nothing. But I'll tell you how I got it. It was just like this. The Germans had us fair, as I tell you, and they shut us up in a barn in the village; just flung us on the ground and left us to starve seemingly. They barred up the big door of the barn, and put a sentry there, and thought we were all right.

'There were sort of slits like very narrow windows in one of the walls, and on the second day it was, I was looking out of these slits down the street, and I could see those German devils were up to mischief. They were planting their machine guns everywhere handy where an ordinary man coming up the street would never see them, but I see them, and I see the infantry lining up behind the garden walls. Then I had a sort of a notion of what was coming; and presently, sure enough, I could hear some of our chaps singing "Hullo, hullo, hullo!" in the distance; and I says to myself, "Not this time."

'So I looked about me, and I found a hole under the wall; a kind of drain I should think it was, and I found I could just squeeze through. And I got out and crept round, and away I goes running down the street, yelling for all I was worth, just as our chaps were getting round the corner at the bottom. "Bang, bang!" went the guns, behind me and in front of me, and on each side of me, and then – bash! something hit me on the head and over I went; and I don't remember anything more till I woke up here just now.'

The soldier lay back in his chair and closed his eyes for a moment. When he opened them he saw that there were other people in the room besides the minister in the black robes. One was a man in a big black cloak. He had a grim old face and a great beaky nose. He shook the soldier by the hand.

'By God! sir,' he said, 'you're a credit to the British Army; you're a damned fine soldier and a good man, and, by God! I'm proud to shake hands with you.'

And then someone came out of the shadow, someone in queer clothes such as the soldier had seen worn by the heralds when he had been on duty at the opening of Parliament by the King.

'Now, by Corpus Domini,' this man said, 'of all knights ye be noblest and gentlest, and ye be of fairest report, and now ye be a brother of the noblest brotherhood that ever was since this world's beginning, since ye have yielded dear life for your friends' sake.'

The soldier did not understand what the man was saying to him. There were others, too, in strange dresses, who came and spoke to him. Some spoke in what sounded like French. He could not make it out; but he knew that they all spoke kindly and praised him.

'What does it all mean?' he said to the minister. 'What are they talking about? They don't think I'd let down my pals?'

'Drink this,' said the minister, and he handed the soldier a great silver cup, brimming with wine.

The soldier took a deep draught, and in that moment all his sorrows passed from him.

'What is it?' he asked.

'Vin nouveau du Royaume,' said the minister. 'New Wine of the Kingdom, you call it.' And then he bent down and murmured in the soldier's ear.

'What,' said the wounded man, 'the place they used to tell us about in Sunday School? With such drink and such joy –'

His voice was hushed. For as he looked at the minister the fashion of his vesture was changed. The black robe seemed to melt away from him. He was all in armour, if armour be made of starlight, of the rose of dawn, and of sunset fires; and he lifted up a great sword of flame.

> Full in the midst, his Cross of Red
> Triumphant Michael brandished,
> And trampled the Apostate's pride.

C. E. MONTAGUE

Charles Edward Montague (1867–1928) was a noted journalist, novelist and critic associated with the Manchester *Guardian*. At the outbreak of the First World War he was over-age but dyed his hair and enrolled as a private. After an injury during bomb-practice he went to France with the Royal Fusiliers in 1915 but his health declined and he was invalided home. The following year he was out again as an intelligence officer, a guide to distinguished visitors and an assistant press censor.

His writings were varied and always contained a touch of humour. *A Trade Report Only* combines both humour and his knowledge of the conditions of war in depicting an eerie situation during one of those moments on the front when the fog drifted over the battlefield and the silence of the tomb prevailed.

9 · A TRADE REPORT ONLY

No one has said what was wrong with The Garden, nor even why it was called by that name: whether because it had apples in it, and also a devil, like Eden; or after Gethsemane and the agonies there; or, again, from Proserpine's garden, because of the hush filling the foreground. All the air near you seemed like so much held breath, with the long rumble of far-away guns stretching out beyond it like some dreamful line of low hills in the distance of a landscape.

The rest of the Western Front has been well written up – much too well. The Garden alone – the Holy Terror, as some of the men used to call it – has not. It is under some sort of taboo. I think I know why. If you were

117

in the line there before the smash came and made it like everywhere else, you could not know how it would work on the nerves when it was still its own elfish self. And if you were there and did know, then you knew also that it was no good to try to tell people. They only said, 'Oh, so you all had the wind up?' We had. But who could say why? How is a horse to say what it is that bedevils one empty place more than another? He has to prick up his ears when he gets there. Then he starts sweating. That's all he knows, and it was the same story with us in The Garden. All I can do is to tell you, just roughly, the make of the place, the way that the few honest solids and liquids were fixed that came into it. They were the least part of it, really.

It was only an orchard, to look at; all ancient apple-trees, dead straight in the stem, with fat, wet grass underneath, a little unhealthy in colour for want of more sun. Six feet above ground the lowest apple boughs all struck out level, and kept so; some beasts, gone in our time, must have eaten every leaf that tried to grow lower. So the under side of the boughs made a sort of flat awning or roof. We called the layer of air between it and the ground The Six-foot Seam, as we were mostly miners. The light in this seam always appeared to have had something done to it: sifted through branches, refracted, messed about somehow, it was not at all the stuff you wanted just at that time. You see the like of it in an eclipse, when the sun gives a queer wink at the earth round the edge of a black mask. Very nice, too, in its place; but the war itself was quite enough out of the common – falling skies all over the place, and half your dead certainties shaken.

We and the Germans were both in The Garden, and knew it. But nobody showed. Everywhere else on the front somebody showed up at last; somebody fired. But here nothing was seen or heard, ever. You found you were whispering and walking on tip-toe, expecting you didn't know what. Have you been in a great crypt at twilight under a church, nothing round you but endless thin pillars, holding up a low roof? Suppose there's a wolf at the far end of the crypt and you alone at the other, staring and staring into the thick of the pillars, and wondering, wondering – round which of the pillars will that grey nose come rubbing?

Why not smash up the silly old spell, you may say – let a good yell, loose a shot, do any sane thing to break out? That's what I said till we got there. Our unit took over the place from the French. A French platoon sergeant, my opposite number, showed me the quarters and posts and the like, and I asked the usual question, 'How's the old Boche?'

'*Mais assez gentil,*' he pattered. That Gaul was not waiting to chat. While he showed me the bomb-store, he muttered something low, hurried, and blurred – '*Le bon Dieu Boche,*' I think it was, had created the orchard. The Germans themselves were '*bons bourgeois*' enough, for all he had seen or heard of them – 'Not a shot in three weeks. *Seulement*' – he grinned, half-shamefaced and half-confidential, as sergeant to sergeant – '*ne faut pas les embeter*'.

I knew all about that. French sergeants were always like that: dervishes in a fight when it came, but dead set, at all other times, on living *paisiblement*, smoking their pipes. *Paisiblement* – they love the very feel of the word in their mouths. Our men were no warrior race, but they all hugged the belief that they really were marksmen, not yet found out by the world. They would be shooting all night at clods, at tops of posts, at anything that might pass for a head. Oh, I knew. Or I thought so.

But no. Not a shot all the night. Nor on any other night either. We were just sucked into the hush of The Garden the way your voice drops in a church – when you go in at the door you become part of the system. I tried to think why. Did nobody fire just because in that place it was so easy for anybody to kill? No trench could be dug; it would have filled in an hour with water filtering through from the full stream flanking The Garden. Sentries stood out among the fruit trees, behind little breastworks of sods, like the things you use to shoot grouse. These screens were merely a form; they would scarcely have slowed down a bullet. They were not defences, only symbols of things that were real elsewhere. Everything else in the place was on queer terms with reality; so were they.

Our first event was the shriek. It was absolutely detached, unrelated to anything seen or heard before or soon after, just like the sudden fall of a great tree on a windless day. At three o'clock on a late autumn morning, a calm moonless night, the depths of The Garden in front of our posts yielded a long wailing scream. I was making a round of our posts at the time, and the scream made me think of a kind of dream I had twice or thrice; not a story dream, but a portrait dream; just a vivid rending vision of the face of some friend with a look on it that made me feel the brute I must have been to have never seen how he or she had suffered, and how little I had known or tried to know. I could not have fancied before that one yell could tell such a lot about anyone. Where it came from there must be some kind of hell going on that went beyond all the hells now in the books, like one of the stars that are still out of sight because the world has not lived long enough to give time for the first ray of light from their blaze to come through to our eyes.

I found the sentries jumpy. 'What is it, sergeant?' one of them almost demanded of me, as if I were the fellow in charge of the devils. 'There's no one on earth,' he said, 'could live in that misery.'

Toomey himself, the red-headed gamekeeper out of the County Fermanagh, betrayed some perturbation. He hinted that 'Them wans' were in it. 'Who?' I asked. 'Ach, the Good People,' he said, with a trace of reluctance. Then I remembered, from old days at school, that the Greeks, too, had been careful; they called their Furies 'The Well-disposed Ladies'.

All the rest of the night there was not a sound but the owls. The sunless day that followed was quiet till 2.30 p.m., when the Hellhound appeared. He came trotting briskly out of the orchard, rounding stem after stem of the fruit trees, leapt our little pretence of barbed wire, and made straight for Toomey, then on guard, as any dog would. It was a young male black-and-tan. It adored Toomey till three, when he was relieved. Then it came capering around him in ecstasy, back to the big living cellar, a hundred yards in the rear. At the door it heard voices within and let down its tail, ready to plead lowliness and contrition before any tribunal less divine than Toomey.

The men, or most of them, were not obtrusively divine just then. They were out to take anything ill that might come. All the hushed days had first drawn their nerves tight, and then the scream had cut some of them. All bawled or squeaked in the cellar, to try to feel natural after the furtive business outside.

'Gawd a'mighty!' Looker shrilled at the entry of Toomey, 'if Fritz ain't sold 'im a pup!'

Jeers flew from all parts of the smoky half-darkness. 'Where's licence, Toomey?'

'Sure 'e's clean in th' 'ouse?'

"Tain't no Dogs' 'Ome 'ere. Over the way!'

Corporal Mullen, the ever-friendly, said to Toomey, more mildly, 'Wot? Goin' soft?'

'A daycent dog, corp,' said Toomey. 'He's bruk wi' the Kaiser. An' I'll engage he's through the distemper. Like as not he'll be an Alsatian.'

Toomey retailed these commendations slowly, with pauses between, to let them sink in.

'What'll you feed him?' asked Mullen, inspecting the points of the beast with charity.

'Feed 'im!' Looker squealed. 'Feed 'im into th' incinerator!'

Toomey turned on him. 'Aye, an' be et be the rats!'

'Fat lot o' talk about rats,' growled Brunt, the White Hope, the company's only prize-fighter. 'Tha'd think rats were struttin' down fairway, shovin' folk off duck-board.'

'Ah!' Looker agreed. 'An' roostin' up yer armpit.'

'Thot's reet,' said Brunt.

'I'll bet 'arf a dollar,' said Looker, eyeing the Hellhound malignantly, 'the 'Uns 'ave loaded him up with plague fleas. Sent 'im acroise. Wiv instructions.'

Toomey protested. 'Can't ye see the dog has been hit, ye blind man?' In fact, the immigrant kept his tail licking expressively under his belly except when it lifted under the sunshine of Toomey's regard.

Brunt rumbled out slow gloomy prophecies from the gloom of his corner. "E'll be tearin' 'imself t'bits wi' t'mange in a fortneet. Rat for breakfas', rat for dinner, rat for tea; bit o' rat las' thaing at neet, 'fore 'e'll stretch down to 't.'

'An' that's the first sinse ye've talked,' Toomey conceded. 'A rotten diet-sheet is ut. An' dirt! An' no kennel the time the roof'll start drippin'. A dog's life for a man, an' God knows what for a dog.'

We felt the force of that. We all had dogs at home. The Hellhound perhaps felt our ruth in the air like a rise of temperature, for at this point he made a couple of revolutions on his wheel base, to get the pampas grass of his imagination comfortable about him, and then collapsed in a curve and lay at rest with his nose to the ground and two soft enigmatic gleams from his eyes raking the twilight recesses of our dwelling. For the moment he was relieved of the post of nucleus-in-chief for the vapours of fractiousness to condense upon.

He had a distinguished successor. The company sergeant-major, no less, came round about five minutes after with 'word from the colonel'. Some mischief all our hearts told us at once. They were right too. The Corps had sent word – just what it would, we inwardly groaned. The Corps had sent word that GHQ – Old GHQ! At it again! we savagely thought. We knew what was coming. Yes GHQ wanted to know what German unit was opposite to us. That meant a raid, of course. The colonel couldn't help it. Like all sane men below brigade staffs, he hated raids. But orders were orders. He did all he could. He sent word that if anyone brought in a German, dead or alive, on his own, by this time tomorrow, he, the colonel, would give him a fiver. Of course nobody could, but it was an offer, meant decently.

Darkness and gnashing of teeth, grunts and snarls of disgust, filled the cellar the moment the CSM had departed. 'Gawd 'elp us!' 'A ride! In The Gawden!' ''Oo says Gawd made gawdens?' 'Ow! Everythink in The Gawden is lovely!' 'Come into The Gawden, Maud!' You see, the wit of most of us was not a weapon of precision. Looker came nearest, perhaps, to the point. 'As if we 'ad a chawnce,' he said, 'to gow aht rattin' Germans, wiv a sack!'

'We gotten dog for't ahl reet,' said Brunt. This was the only audible trace of good humour. Toomey looked at Brunt quickly.

Toomey was destined to trouble that afternoon; one thing came after another. At 3.25 I sent him and Brunt, with a clean sack apiece, to the sergeant-major's dug-out for the rations. They came back in ten minutes. As Toomey gave me his sack, I feared that I saw a thin train of mixed black and white dust trending across the powdered mortar floor to the door. Then I saw Looker, rage in his face, take a candle and follow this trail, stooping down, and once tasting the stuff on a wet finger-tip.

And then the third storm burst. 'Christ!' Looker yelled. 'If 'e ain't put the tea in the sack wiv a 'ole in it!'

We all knew that leak in a bottom corner of that special sack as we knew every very small thing in our life of small things – the cracked dixie-lid, the brazier's short leg, the way that Mynns had of clearing his throat, and Brunt of working his jaws before spitting. Of course, the sack was all right for loaves and the tinned stuff. But tea! – loose tea mixed with powdered sugar! It was like loading a patent seed-sowing machine with your fortune in gold-dust. There was a general groan of 'God help us!' with extras. In this report I leave out, all along, a great many extras. Print and paper are dear.

Looker was past swearing. 'Plyin' a piper-chise!' he ejaculated with venom. 'All owver Frawnce! Wiv our grub!'

Toomey was sorely distressed. He, deep in whose heart was lodged the darling vision of Toomey the managing head, the contriver, the 'oul lad that was in ut', had bungled a job fit for babes. 'Ah, then, who could be givin' his mind to the tea,' he almost moaned, 'an' he with a grand thought in ut?'

At any other time and place the platoon would have settled down, purring, under those words. 'A grand thought', 'a great idaya' – when Toomey in happier days had owned to being in labour with one of these heirs of his invention, some uncovenanted mercy had nearly always accrued before long to his friends – a stew of young rabbits, two brace of fat pheasants, once a mighty wild goose. The tactician, we understood in a general way, had 'put the comether upon' them. Now even those delicious memories were turned to gall. 'Always the sime!' Looker snarled at the fallen worker of wonders. 'Always the sime! Ye cawn't 'ave a bit o' wire sived up for pipe-cleanin' without 'e'll loan it off yer to go snarin' 'ares.' Looker paused for a moment, gathering all the resources of wrath, and then he swiftly scaled the high top-gallant of ungraciousness: "E wiv the 'ole platoon workin' awye for 'im, pluckin' pawtridge an' snipes, the 'ole wye up from the sea! Top end o' Frawnce is all amuck o' feathers wiv 'im!'

All were good men; Looker, like Toomey, a very good man. It was only their nerves that had gone, and the jolly power of gay and easy relentment after a jar. However they tried, they could not cease yapping. I went out for a drink of clean air. If you are to go on loving mankind, you must take a rest from it sometimes. As I went up the steps from the cellar the rasping jangle from below did not cease; it only sank on my ears as I went. 'Ow, give us 'Owm Rule for England, Gord's sike!' 'Sye there ain't no towds in Irelan', do they?' 'Looker, I've tould you I'm sorry, an' –' 'Garn, both on yer! Ol' gas-projectors!' 'Begob, if ye want an eye knocked from ye then – !' I was going back, but then I heard Corporal Mullen, paternal and firm, like Neptune rebuking the winds. 'Now, then, we don't none of us want to go losing our heads about nothing.' No need to trouble, Mullen would see to the children.

I went east, into The Garden. Ungathered apples were going to loss on its trees. I stood looking at one of them for a time, and then it suddenly detached itself and fell to the ground with a little thud and a splash of squashed brown rottenness, as if my eye had plucked it. After that sound the stillness set in again: stillness of autumn, stillness of vigilant fear, and now the stillness of oncoming evening, the nun, to make it more cloistral. No silence so deep but that it can be deepened! As minutes passed, infinitesimal whispers – I think from mere wisps of eddies, twisting round snags in the stream – began to lift into hearing. Deepening silence is only the rise into clearness, of this or that more confidential utterance.

I must have been sucking that confidence in for a good twenty minutes before I turned with a start. I had to, I did not know why. It seemed as if some sense, which I did not know I had got, told me that someone was stealing up behind me. No one there; nothing but Arras, the vacuous city, indistinct among her motionless trees. She always seemed to be listening and frightened. It was as if the haggard creature had stirred.

I looked to my front again, rather ashamed. Was I losing hold too? I wondered as I gazed level out into the Seam and watched the mist deepening. Each evening that autumn, a quilt of very white mist would come out of the soaked soil of The Garden, lay itself out, flat and dense, but shallow at first, over the grass, and then deepen upward as twilight advanced, first submerging the tips of the grass and the purple snake-headed flowers; and then thickening steadily up till the whole Six-foot Seam was packed with milky opaqueness.

Sixty yards out from our front a heron was standing, immobilized, in the stream, staring down – for a last bit of fishing no doubt. As I watched him, his long head came suddenly round and half up. He listened. He stood like that, warily, for a minute, then seemed to decide it was no place for him, hoisted himself off the ground, and winged slowly away with great flaps. I felt cold, and thought, 'What a time I've been loafing round here!' But I found it was four o'clock only. I thought I would go on and visit my sentries, the three o'clock men who would come off duty at five. It would warm me; and one or two of the young ones were apt to be creepy about sundown.

Schofield, the lad in one of our most advanced posts, was waist-deep in the mist when I reached him.

'Owt, boy?' I whispered. He was a North Country man.

'Nowt, sergeant,' he answered, 'barrin' –' He checked. He was one of the stout ones you couldn't trust to yell out for help if the Devil were at them.

'What's wrong?' I asked pretty sharply.

'Nobbut t'way,' he said slowly, 'they deucks doan't seem t'be gettin' down to it to-neet.' My eye followed his through the boughs to the pallid sky. A flight of wild duck were whirling and counter-whirling aloft in some odd *pas d'inquietude*. Yes; no doubt our own ducks that had come during the war, with the herons and snipe, to live in The Garden, the untrodden marsh where, between the two lines of rifles never unloaded, no shot was ever heard and snipe were safe from all snipers. A good lad, Schofield; he took a lot of notice of things. But what possessed the creatures? What terror infested their quarters tonight?

I looked Schofield over. He was as near to dead white as a tanned man can come – that is, a bad yellow. But he could be left. A man that keeps on taking notice of things he can see, instead of imagining ones that he can't, is a match for the terror that walketh by twilight. I stole on to our most advanced post of all. There I was not so sure of my man. He was Mynns. We call him Billy Wisdom, because he was a schoolmaster in civil life – some council school at Hoggerston. 'What cheer, Billy?' I whispered. 'Anything to report?'

The mist was armpit deep on him now, but the air quite clear above that, so that from three feet off I saw his head and shoulders well, and his bayonet; nothing else at all. He did not turn when I spoke, nor unfix his eyes from the point he had got them set on, in front of his post and a little below their own level. 'All – quiet – and – correct – sergeant,' he said, as if each word were a full load and had to be hauled by itself. I had once seen a man drop his rifle and bolt back overland from his post, to trial and execution and anything rather than that everlasting wait for a bayonet's point to come lunging up out of thick mist in front and a little below him, into the gullet, under the chin. Billy was near bolting-point, I could tell by more senses than one. He was losing hold on one bodily function after another, but still hanging on hard to something, some grip of the spirit that held from second to second, after muscle had mutinied and nerve was gone.

He had hardly spoken before a new torment wrung him. The whole landscape suddenly gave a quick shiver. The single poplar down the stream just perceptibly shuddered and rustled, and then was dead still again. A bed of rushes, nearer us, swayed for an instant, and stood taut again. Absurd, you will say. And, of course, it was only a faint breath of wind, the only stir in the air all that day. But you were not there. So you cannot feel how the cursed place had tried to shake itself free of its curse, and had failed and fallen rigid again, dreeing its weird, and poor Billy with it. His hold on his tongue was what he lost now. He began to wail under his breath, 'Christ, pity me! Oh, suffering Christ, pity me!' He was still staring hard to his front, but I had got a hand ready to grab at his belt when, from somewhere out in the mist before us, there came, short and crisp, the crack of a dead branch heavily trodden upon.

Billy was better that instant. Better an audible enemy, one with a body, one that could trample on twigs, than that vague infestation of life with impalpable sinisterness. Billy turned with a grin – ghastly enough, but a grin.

'Hold your fire,' I said in his ear, 'till I order.' I made certain dispositions of bombs on a little shelf. Then we waited, listening, second by second. I think both our ears must have flicked like a mule's. But the marvel came in at the eye. We both saw the vision at just the same instant. It was some fifty yards from us, straight to our front. It sat on the top of the mist as though mist were ice and would bear. It was a dog, of the very same breed as the Hellhound, sitting upright like one of the beasts that support coats-of-arms; all proper too, as the heralds would say, with the black and tan hues as in life. The image gazed at us fixedly. How long? Say, twenty seconds. Then it about-turned without any visible use of its limbs, and receded some ten or twelve yards, still sitting up and now rhythmically rising and falling as though the mist it rode upon were undulating. Then it clean vanished. I thought it sank, as if the mist had ceased to bear. Billy thought the beast just melted into the air radially, all round, as rings made of smoke.

You know the crazy coolness, a sort of false presence of mind, that will come in and fool you a little bit further at these moments of staggering dislocation of cause and effect. One of these waves of mad rationalism broke on me now. I turned quickly round to detect the cinema lantern behind us which must have projected the dog's moving figure upon the white sheet of mist. None there, of course. Only the terrified city, still there, aghast, with held breath.

Then all my anchors gave together. I was adrift; there was nothing left certain. I thought, 'What if all we are sure of be just a mistake, and our sureness about it conceit, and we no better than puppies ourselves to wonder that dogs should be taking their ease in mid-air and an empty orchard be shrieking?' While I was drifting, I happened to notice the sleepy old grumble of guns from the rest of the front, and I envied those places. Sane, normal places; happy all who were there; only their earthworks were crumbling, not the last few certainties that we men think we have got hold of.

All this, of course, had to go on in my own mind behind a shut face. For Billy was one of the nerve specialists; he might get a VC, or be shot in a walled yard at dawn, according to how he was handled. So I was pulling my wits together a little, to dish out some patter fit for his case – you know: the 'bright, breezy, brotherly' bilge – when the next marvel came. A sound this time – a voice, too; no shriek, not even loud, but tranquil, articulate, slow, and so distant that only the deathly stillness which gave high relief to every bubble that burst with a plop, out in the marsh, could bring the words to us at all. 'Has annywan here lost a dog? Annywan lost a good dog? Hoond? Goot Hoond? Annywan lost a goot hoond?'

You never can tell how things will take you. I swear I was right out of that hellish place for a minute or more, alive and free and back at home among the lost delights of Epsom Downs, between the races; the dear old smelly crowd all over the course, and the merchant who carries a tray crying, "Oo'll 'ave a good cigar, gents? Two pence! 'Oo wants a good cigar? Two pence! 'Oo says a good smoke?' And the sun shining good on all the bookies and crooks by the rails, the just and the unjust, all jolly and natural. Better than Lear's blasted heath and your mind running down!

You could see the relief settle on Mynns like oil going on to a burn on your hand. Have you seen an easy death in bed? – the yielding sigh of peace and the sinking inwards, the weary job over? It was like that. He breathed 'That Irish swine!' in a voice that made it a blessing. I felt the same, but more uneasily. One of my best was out there in the wide world, having God knew what truck with the enemy. Any Brass Hat that came loafing round might think, in his blinded soul, that Toomey was fraternizing; whereas Toomey was dead or prisoner by now, or as good, unless delivered by some miracle of gumption surpassing all his previous practices against the brute creation. We could do nothing, could not even guess where he was in the fog. It had risen right up to the boughs; the whole Seam was packed with it, tight. No one but he who had put his head into the mouth of the tiger could pull it out now.

We listened on, with pricked ears. Voices we certainly heard; yes, more than one, but not a word clear. And voices were not what I harked for – it was for the shot that would be the finish of Toomey. I remembered during the next twenty minutes quite a lot of good points about Toomey. I found that I had never had a sulky word from him, for one. At the end of the twenty minutes the voices finally stopped. But no shot came. A prisoner, then?

The next ten minutes were bad. Towards the end of the two hours for which they lasted I could have fancied the spook symptoms were starting again. For out of the mist before us there came something that was not seen, or heard, or felt; no one sense could fasten upon it; only a mystic consciousness came of some approaching displacement of the fog. The blind, I believe, feel the same when they come near a lamp-post. Slowly this undefined source of impressions drew near, from out the uncharted spaces beyond to the frontiers of hearing and sight, slipped across them and took form, at first as the queerest tangle of two sets of limbs, and then as Toomey, bearing on one shoulder a large corpse, already stiff, clothed in field-grey.

'May I come in, sergeant?' said Toomey, 'an' bring me sheaves wid me?' The pride of 'cuteness shone from his eyes like a lamp through the fog; his voice had the urbanely affected humility of the consciously great.

'You may,' said I, 'if you've given nothing away.'

'I have not,' said he. 'I'm an importer entirely. Me exports are nil.' He rounded the flank of the breastwork and laid the body tenderly down, as a collector would handle a Strad. 'There wasn't the means of an identification about me. Me shoulder titles, me badge, me pay-book, me small-book, me disc, an' me howl correspondence – I left all beyant in the cellar. They'd not have got value that tuk me.' Toomey's face was all one wink. To value himself on his courage would never enter his head. It was the sense of the giant intellect within that filled him with triumph.

I inspected the bulging eyes of the dead. 'Did you strangle him sitting?' I asked.

'Not at all. Amn't I just after tradin' the dog for him?' Then, in the proper whisper, Toomey made his report:

'Ye'll remember the whillabalooin' there was at meself in the cellar. Leppin' they were, at the loss of the tea. The end of it was that "I'm goin' out now," said I, "to speak to a man," said I, "about a dog", an' I quitted the place, an' the dog with me, knockin' his nose against every lift of me heel. I'd a grand thought in me head, to make them whisht thinkin' bad of me. Very near where the lad Schofiel' is, I set out for Germ'ny, stoopin' low, to get all the use of the fog. Did you notus me, sergeant?'

'Breaking the firewood?' I said.

'Aye, I med sure that ye would. So I signalled.'

Now I perceived. Toomey went on. 'I knew, when I held up the dog on the palm of me hand, ye'd see where I was, an' where goin'. Then I wint on, deep into th' East. Their wire is nothin' at all; it's the very spit of our own. I halted among ut, and gev out a notus, in English an' Gemnan, keepin' well down in fog to rejuce me losses. They didn't fire – ye'll have heard that. They sint for the man with the English. An', be the will o' God, he was the same man that belonged to the dog.

' "Hans," says I, courcheous but firm, "the dog is well off where he is. Will you come to him quietly?"

'I can't jus' give ye his wods, but the sinse of them only. "What are ye doin' at all," he says, "askin' a man to desert?"

'There was serious trouble in that fellow's voice. It med me ashamed. But I wint on, an' only put double strength in me temptin's. "Me colonel," I told him, "is offerin' five pounds for a prisoner. Come back with me now and ye'll have fifty francs for yourself when I get the reward. Think over ut well. Fifty francs down. There's a grand lot of spendin' in that. An' ye'll be wi' the dog." As I offered him each injucement, I lifted th' an'mal clear of the fog for two seconds or three, to keep the man famished wid longin'. You have to be crool in a war. Each time that I lowered the dog I lep' two paces north, under the fog, to be-divvil their aim if they fired.

' "Ach, to hell wi' your francs an' your pounds," says he in his ag'ny. "Give me the dog or I'll shoot. I see where you are."

' "I'm not there at all," says I, "an' the dog's in front of me bosom."

'Ye'll understan', sergeant,' Toomey said to me gravely, 'that last was a ruse. I'd not do the like o' that to a dog, anny more than yourself.

'The poor divvil schewed in his juice for a while, very quiet. Then he out with an offer. "Will ye take sivinty francs for the dog? It's the whole of me property. An' it only comes short be five francs of th' entire net profuts ye'd make on the fiver, an' I comin' with you."

' "I will not," says I, faint and low. It was tormint refusin' the cash.

' "Won't *annythin'* do ye," says he in despair, "but a live man?"

' "Depinds," says I pensively, playin' me fish. I held up the dog for a second again, to keep his sowl workin'.

'He plunged, at the sight of the creature. "Couldn't ye do with a body?"

he says very low.

' "Depends," says I, marvellin' was ut a human sacrifice he was for makin', the like of the Druids, to get back the dog.

' "Not fourteen hours back," says he, "he died on us."

' "Was he wan of yourselves?" says I. "A nice fool I'd look if I came shankin' back from the fair wid a bit of the wrong unit."

' "He was," says he, "an' the best of us all." An' then he went on, wid me puttin' in just a word now and then, or a glimpse of the dog, to keep him desirous and gabbin'. There's no use in cheapenin' your wares. He let on how this fellow he spoke of had never joyed since they came to that place, an' gone mad at the finish wi' not gettin' his sleep without he'd be seein' Them Wans in a dream and hearin' the Banshies; the way he bruk out at three in the morning that day, apt to cut anny in two that would offer to hold him. "Here's out of it all," he appeared to have said; "I've lived through iv'ry room in hell, how long, O Lord, how long, but it's glory an' victory now," an' off an' away wid him West, through The Garden. "Ye'll not have seen him at all?" says me friend. We hadn't notussed, I told him. "We were right then," says he; "he'll have died on the way. For he let a scream in the night that a man couldn't give an' live after. If he'd fetched up at your end," says he, "you'd have known, for he was a brave as a lion."

' "A livin' dog's better," says I, "than anny dead lion. It's a Jew's bargain you're makin'! Where's the deceased?"

' "Pass me the dog," says he, "an' I'll give you his route out from here to where he'll have dropped. It's his point of deparchure I stand at."

' "I'll come to ye there," says I, "an' ye'll give me his bearin's, an' when I've set eyes on me man I'll come back an' hand ye the dog, an' not sooner."

'He was spaichless a moment. "Come now," says I, from me lair in the fog, "wan of the two of us has to be trustful. I'll not let ye down."

' "Ye'll swear to come back?" says he in great anguish.

'I said, "Tubbe sure."

' "Come on with ye, then," he answered.

'I went stoopin' along to within six feet of his voice, the way ye'd swim under water, an' then I came to the surface. The clayey-white face that he had, an' the top of his body showed over a breastwork the moral of ours. An', be cripes, it was all right. The red figures were plain on his shoulder-strap – wan-eighty-six. Another breastwork the fellow to his was not thirty yards south. There was jus' the light left me to see that the sentry there was wan-eighty-six too. I'd inspicted the goods in bulk now, an' only had to see to me sample an' off home with it.'

Toomey looked benedictively down on the long stiff frame with its Iron Cross ribbon and red worsted '186'. 'An ould storm-trooper!' Toomey commendingly said. 'His friend gev me the line to him. Then he got anxious. "Ye'll bury him fair?" he said. "Is he a Prod'stant?" says I, "or a Cath'lic?" "A good Cath'lic," says he; "we're Bavarians here." "Good," says I, "I'll speak to Father Moloney meself." "An' ye'll come back," says he, "wi' the dog?" "I will not," says I, "I shall hand him ye now. Ye're a straight man not to ha' shot me before. Besides, ye're a Cath'lic?" So I passed him the an'mal and off on me journey. Not the least trouble at all, findin' the body. The birds were all pointin' to ut. They hated ut. Faith, but that fellow had seen the quare things!' Toomey looked down again at the monstrously staring eyes of his capture, bursting with agonies more fantastic, I thought, than any that stare from the bayoneted dead in a trench.

'The man wi' the dog,' Toomey said, 'may go the same road. His teeth are all knockin' together. A match for your own, Billy.' In trenches you did not pretend not to know all about one another, the best and the worst. In that screenless life friendship frankly condoled with weak nerves or an ugly face or black temper.

'Sergeant,' said Toomey, 'ye'll help me indent for the fiver? A smart drop of drink it'll be for the whole of the boys.'

I nodded. 'Bring him along,' I said, 'now.'

'Well, God ha' mercy on his sowl,' said Toomey, hoisting the load on to his back.

'And of all Christian souls, I pray God.' I did not say it. Only Ophelia's echo, crossing my mind. How long would Mynns last? Till I could wangle his transfer to the divisional laundry or gaff?

I brought Toomey along to claim the fruit of his guile. We had to pass Schofield. He looked more at ease in his mind than before. I asked the routine question. 'All correct, sergeant,' he answered. 'Deucks is coom dahn. Birds is all stretchin' dahn to it, proper.'

Its own mephitic mock-peace was refilling The Garden. But no one can paint a miasma. Anyhow, I am not trying to. This is a trade report only.

ROBERT BLOCH

Robert Bloch (1917–   ), the Chicago born writer of horror and fantasy stories, needs no introduction. He sold his first story, *The Feast in the Abbey*, at the age of seventeen to *Weird Tales* and continued to write in his spare time until film director Alfred Hitchcock filmed Bloch's *Psycho*. He is now one of the greatest names in the field but far too few of his works have a military setting.

Strategy is as important in an offensive as fire-power or any other factor. Many important and ingenious stratagems were used by both sides in the Second World War and to the long list of code-names used could well be added Operation Vampire if the following were true. One wonders if the use of a vampire, as recounted in *The Living Dead*, by the German army might not be a very risky business to all concerned.

10 · THE LIVING DEAD

ALL day long he rested, while the guns thundered in the village below. Then in the slanting shadows of the late afternoon, the rumbling echoes faded into the distance and he knew it was over. The American advance had crossed the river. They were gone at last, and it was safe once more.

Above the village, in the crumbling ruins of the château atop the wooded hillside, Count Barsac emerged from the crypt.

The Count was tall and thin – cadaverously thin, in a manner most hideously appropriate. His face and hands had a waxen pallor, his hair was dark, but not as dark as his eyes and the hollows beneath them. His cloak was black, and the sole touch of colour about his person was the vivid redness of his lips when they curled in a smile.

He was smiling now, in the twilight, for it was time to play the game.

The name of the game was Death, and the Count had played it many times.

He had played it in Paris on the stage of the Grand Guignol; his name had been plain Eric Karon then, but still he'd won a certain renown for his interpretation of bizarre roles. Then the war had come and, with it, his opportunity.

Long before the Germans took Paris, he'd joined their Underground, working long and well. As an actor he'd been invaluable.

And this, of course, was his ultimate reward – to play the supreme role, not on the stage, but in real life. To play without the artifice of spotlights, in true darkness; this was the actor's dream come true. He had even helped to fashion the plot.

'Simplicity itself,' he told his German superiors. 'Château Barsac has been deserted since the Revolution. None of the peasants from the village dare to venture near it, even in daylight because of the legend. It is said, you see, that the last Count Barsac was a vampire.'

And so it was arranged. The short-wave transmitter had been set up in the large crypt beneath the château, with three skilled operators in attendance, working in shifts. And he, 'Count Barsa,' in charge of the entire operation, as guardian angel. Rather, as guardian demon.

'There is a graveyard on the hillside below,' he informed them. 'A humble resting place for poor and ignorant people. It contains a single imposing crypt – the ancestral tomb of the Barsacs. We shall open that crypt, remove the remains of the last Count, and allow the villagers to discover that the coffin is empty. They will never dare come near the spot or the château again, because this will prove that the legend is true – Count Barsac is a vampire, and walks once more.'

The question came then. 'What if there are sceptics? What if someone does not believe?'

And he had his answer ready. 'They will believe. For at night I shall walk – I, Count Barsac.'

After they saw him in the make-up, wearing the black cloak, there were no more questions. The role was his.

The role was his, and he'd played it well. The Count nodded to himself as he climbed the stairs and entered the roofless foyer of the château, where only a configuration of cobwebs veiled the radiance of the rising moon.

Now, of course, the curtain must come down. If the American advance had swept past the village below, it was time to make one's bow and exit. And that too had been well arranged.

During the German withdrawal another advantageous use had been made of the tomb in the graveyard. A cache of Air Marshal Goering's art treasures now rested safely and undisturbed within the crypt. A truck had been placed in the château. Even now the three wireless operators would be playing new parts – driving the truck down the hillside to the tomb, placing the *objets d'art* in it.

By the time the Count arrived there, everything would be packed. They would then don the stolen American Army uniforms, carry the forged identifications and permits, drive through the lines across the river, and rejoin the German forces at a predesignated spot. Nothing had been left to chance. Some day, when he wrote his memoirs. . . .

But there was not time to consider that now. The Count glanced up through the gaping aperture in the ruined roof. The moon was high. It was time to leave.

In a way he hated to go. Where others saw only dust and cobwebs he saw a stage – the setting of his finest performance. Playing a vampire's role had not addicted him to the taste of blood – but as an actor he enjoyed the taste of triumph. And he had triumphed here.

'Parting is such sweet sorrow.' Shakespeare's line. Shakespeare, who had written of ghosts and witches, of bloody apparitions. Because Shakespeare knew that his audiences, the stupid masses believed in such things – just as they still believed today. A great actor could always make them believe.

The Count moved into the shadowy darkness outside the entrance of the château. He started down the pathway towards the beckoning trees.

It was here, amid the trees, that he had come upon Raymond, one evening weeks ago. Raymond had been his most appreciative audience – a stern, dignified, white-haired elderly man, mayor of the village of Barsac. But there had been nothing dignified about the old fool when he'd caught sight of the Count looming up before him out of the night. He'd screamed like a woman and run.

Probably Raymond had been prowling around, intent on poaching, but all that had been forgotten after his encounter in the woods. The mayor was the one to thank for spreading the rumours that the Count was again abroad. He and Clodez, the oafish miller, had then led an armed band to the graveyard and entered the Barsac tomb. What a fright they got when they discovered the Count's coffin open and empty!

The coffin had contained only dust that had been scattered to the winds, but they could not know that. Nor could they know about what happened to Suzanne.

The Count was passing the banks of the small stream now. Here, on another evening, he'd found the girl – Raymond's daughter, as luck would have it – in an embrace with young Antoine LeFevre, her lover. Antoine's shattered leg had invalided him out of the army, but he ran like a deer when he glimpsed the cloaked and grinning Count. Suzanne had been left behind and that was unfortunate, because it was necessary to dispose of her. Her body had been buried in the woods, beneath great stones, and there was no question of discovery; still, it was a regrettable incident.

In the end, however, everything was for the best. Now silly superstitious Raymond was doubly convinced that the vampire walked. He had seen the creature himself, had seen the empty tomb and the open coffin; his own daughter had disappeared. At his command none dared venture near the graveyard, the woods, or the château beyond.

Poor Raymond! He was not even a mayor any more – his village had been destroyed in the bombardment. Just an ignorant, broken old man, mumbling his idiotic nonsense about the 'living dead'.

The Count smiled and walked on, his cloak fluttering in the breeze, casting a bat-like shadow on the pathway before him. He could see the graveyard now, the tilted tombstones rising from the earth like leprous fingers rotting in the moonlight. His smile faded; he did not like such thoughts. Perhaps the greatest tribute to his talent as an actor lay in his actual aversion to death, to darkness and what lurked in the night. He hated the sight of blood, had developed within himself an almost claustrophobic dread of the confinement of the crypt.

Yes, it had been a great role, but he was thankful it was ending. It would be good to play the man once more, and cast off the creature he had created.

As he approached the crypt he saw the truck waiting in the shadows. The entrance to the tomb was open, but no sounds issued from it. That meant his colleagues had completed their task of loading and were ready to go. All that remained now was to change his clothing, remove the make-up and depart.

The Count moved to the darkened truck. And then. . . .

Then they were upon him, and he felt the tines of the pitchfork bite into his back, and as the flash of lanterns dazzled his eyes he heard the stern command. 'Don't move!'

He didn't move. He could only stare as they surrounded him – Antoine, Clodez, Raymond, and the others, a dozen peasants from the village. A dozen armed peasants, glaring at him in mingled rage and fear, holding him at bay.

But how could they dare?

The American Corporal stepped forward. That was the answer, of course – the American Corporal and another man in uniform, armed with a sniper's rifle. They were responsible. He didn't even have to see the riddled corpses of the three short-wave operators piled in the back of the truck to understand what had happened. They'd stumbled on his men while they worked, shot them down, then summoned the villagers.

Now they were jabbering questions at him, in English, of course. He understood English, but he knew better than to reply.

'Who are you? Were these men working under your orders? Where were you going with this truck?'

The Count smiled and shook his head. After a while they stopped, as he knew they would.

The Corporal turned to his companion. 'Okay,' he said. 'Let's go.' The other man nodded and climbed into the cab of the truck as the motor coughed into life. The Corporal moved to join him, then turned to Raymond.

'We're taking this across the river,' he said. 'Hang on to our friend here – they'll be sending a guard detail for him within an hour.'

Raymond nodded.

The truck drove off into the darkness.

And as it was dark now – the moon had vanished behind a cloud. The Count's smile vanished, too, as he glanced around at his captors. A rabble of stupid clods, surly and ignorant. But armed. No chance of escaping. And they kept staring at him, and mumbling.

'Take him to the tomb.'

It was Raymond who spoke, and they obeyed, prodding their captive forward with pitchforks. That was when the Count recognized the first ray of hope. For they prodded him most gingerly, no man coming close, and when he glared at them their eyes dropped.

They were putting him in the crypt because they were afraid of him. Now the Americans were gone, they feared him once more – feared his presence and his power. After all, in their eyes he was a vampire – he might turn into a bat and vanish entirely. So they wanted him in the tomb for safekeeping.

The Count shrugged, smiled his most sinister smile, and bared his teeth. They shrank back as he entered the doorway. He turned and, on impulse, furled his cape. It was an instinctive final gesture, in keeping with his role – and it provoked the appropriate response. They moaned, and old Raymond crossed himself. It was better, in a way, than any applause.

In the darkness of the crypt the Count permitted himself to relax a trifle. He was off stage now. A pity he'd not been able to make his exit the way he'd planned, but such were the fortunes of war. Soon he'd be taken to the American headquarters and interrogated. Undoubtedly there would be some unpleasant moments, but the worst that could befall him was a few months in a prison camp. And even the Americans must bow to him in appreciation when they heard the story of his masterful deception.

It was dark in the crypt, and musty. The Count moved about restlessly. His knee grazed the edge of the empty coffin set on a trestle in the tomb. He shuddered involuntarily, loosening his cape at the throat. It would be good to remove it, good to be out of here, good to shed the role of vampire forever. He'd played it well, but now he was anxious to be gone.

There was a mumbling audible from outside, mingled with another and less identifiable noise – a scraping sound. The Count moved to the closed door of the crypt and listened intently; but now there was only silence.

What were the fools doing out there? He wished the Americans would hurry back. It was too hot in here. And why the sudden silence?

Perhaps they'd gone.

Yes. That was it. The Americans had told them to wait and guard him, but they were afraid. They really believed he was a vampire – old Raymond had convinced them of that. So they'd run off. They'd run off, and he was free, he could escape now. . . .

So the Count opened the door.

And he saw them then, saw them standing and waiting, old Raymond staring sternly for a moment before he moved forward. He was holding something in his hand, and the Count recognized it, remembering the scraping sound that he'd heard.

It was a long wooden stake with a sharp point.

Then he opened his mouth to scream, telling them it was only a trick, he was no vampire, they were a pack of superstitious fools. . . .

But all the while they bore him back into the crypt, lifting him up and thrusting him into the open coffin, holding him there as the grim-faced Raymond raised the pointed stake above his heart.

It was only when the stake came down that he realized there's such a thing as playing a role too well.

SEABURY QUINN

Death is something which comes to us all, sometimes to a soldier sooner than others. But death is inevitable – or is it possible to bring back the dead? This is a tale of a fond mother who did succeed in bringing back her son from the grave – but a man who has been to the gates of Hell and back again is never quite the same again.

The years immediately after the First World War saw very few stories of the supernatural in Britain. The birth of the American magazine *Weird Tales* in 1923 began a new era in the genre. During its first year Seabury Quinn had his first story published and from then until his death at the age of eighty in 1969 he had written over 500 stories. Ninety of these featured the never-to-be-forgotten character, Jules de Grandin – psychic investigator extraordinary, and the remainder explored every facet of the macabre. *And Give Us Yesterday* is the only tale by Quinn which was directly inspired by the Second World War and, as was to be expected, his approach was unique.

11 · AND GIVE US YESTERDAY

For the tenth time Angela picked up the letter from the Quartermaster General with Form 345, Military, enclosed, the four options she might exercise; have him left near the beach where he fell, have him brought back for interment in a private cemetery, have him shipped to some foreign country, or sent back for burial in Arlington. She wanted none of them. She wanted her boy back, her Harold with his neat brown hair that waved a little just above the temples, steady hazel eyes and ready smile that lifted slightly more to the left than the right.

Three years ago when she received the formal notice from the War Department with its facsimile of the Adjutant General's signature she had felt betrayed, desolate, all her high hopes crumbled into fragments at her feet. She hadn't fainted, hadn't cried, but she had bitten her lips till the salty taste of blood was in her mouth as she sat with her hands demurely folded in her lap, all feeling gone from her eyes. She wanted desperately to cry, but there were no tears. She wanted desperately to pray, but couldn't; God seemed somehow terribly unreal. Then, with a feeling all her insides were becoming unfastened – and not the faintest notion what she could do about it – she walked slowly to his bedroom with the Japanese prints on the walls, the scarf of brown-blocked Java linen for a counterpane and her and Darcy's photographs on the dresser. She drew back the door of the closet where his suits draped in orderly array on hangers, tweeds, flannels, worsteds, dress and dinner kits, brown shoes and black on wooden trees set toe to toe, hats neatly brushed and put away in paste-board boxes. A little whiff of peat from Harris tweeds and Shetland weaves came to her, and the faint elusive scent of lavender and Russian leather and tobacco – odours redolent of him as carnation or violet may be of a beloved woman – and, scarce knowing what she did, she drew the sleeve of a camel's hair topcoat round her shoulders, sank her cheek in its soft silky fleece. 'Harold,' she murmured, her voice muffled by the yielding cloth. 'Oh, my boy; my boy!' Then she let her breath out slowly, with an odd jerk in it, as if she had not breathed for a long time and needed practice to pick up the way of it again.

Since that day nothing seemed to matter. 'Thank you, thank you, very much,' she had told the minister, 'Thank you,' to the kind old ladies of the congregation, 'Thank you,' to the laundry-man and grocer and the men who came to read the electric and gas meters, and the tone with which she voiced her thanks was flat, expressionless, almost mechanical. The War Department's citation and the Purple Heart had no more impact on her numbed senses than a fresh blow on a punch-drunk boxer. She ignored the stilted, sloppily typed communications from the Veterans' Administration. What need had she to ask insurance payments or pension? With health, sufficient money, more beauty than a woman in her middle forties had a right to dare hope for, she already had everything – and nothing.

Now, after three years came this latest message from the War Department and her heart that she had thought wrung dry of sorrow refilled itself from memories. She laid the papers down, her slim white fingers smoothing them almost caressingly, and tears slipped in big jewel-bright drops down her cheeks. She didn't sob, not so much as a sigh escaped her; she just sat there in the big twilit room, her face like ivory, letting those big tears run down her cheeks. At last: 'O God,' she murmured, quoting something she had heard or read long, long ago, 'turn back Thy universe and give us yesterday!'

Her lips, as naturally pink as pigeons' feet and needing no rouge to define their perfection, joined in a smile as she finished. Her flexible mouth widened and her cheeks lifted a little; a dimple dented the smooth flesh beside her mouth, her sensitive nostrils expanded – all the components of a smile appeared in her face. But there was no smile. It was, rather, a bitter grimace of derision. 'But that would take a special kind of miracle, of course,' her voice seemed tired, so utterly weary it might have been that of an old woman, 'and miracles like that, are out of date, aren't they? You gave them up after Capernaum and Bethany.' Her acid laughter was a goading echo in the gathering dusk.

Something cool and black, faintly moist, insinuated itself into the hand she let trail idly beside her and a furred foot pawed her arm gently. 'Oh!' she exclaimed, a little startled then, 'Oh, it's you, Mr Chips,' as she looked into the yellow eyes turned pleadingly to hers. 'You want to go for your walk? Very well, go get the lead.'

The honey-coloured cocker trotted off, nails clicking on the polished floor, and Angela rose half reluctantly, half eagerly to carry out the evening rite. Chips had come to them when he was a fist-sized bundle of soft fluffy fur about the shade of a Teddy bear. He had been Harold's dog, selected from a dozen sportive, friendly puppies at a pet shop on Fifth Avenue, and Harold had adored him, pampered him, looked after him from awkward, stumbling puppyhood to sedate middle age. When Harold went away to camp the duty of the daily run – which had slowed to a dignified amble with the years – developed on Angela.

They made a circuit of the square each evening just as dusk was deepening into dark. Chips strained at the lead, hanging back, investigating tree boxes, fire hydrants or the little bare spots of raw earth around the trees with an interrogative black nose, giving vent to subdued snorts of approval or muted whimpers of disfavour at what he discovered. Angela indulged him for as long as seemed reasonable, then her sharp, 'That's quite enough, Chips,' brought him from his olfactory researches, and he would trot sedately beside her till fresh locations roused the latent archaeologist in him again. In this way they effected complete encompassment of the Square, each occupied with his own thoughts, each tolerant of the other's privacy, as became gentle-folk, whether canine or human.

The air that flowed through the French windows of the drawing-room bore a faint mingled scent of flowers, new-mown grass and recently washed asphalt as she snapped the snaffle of the lead to the dog's harness and made for the street. Van Nostrand Square was like an etching in the July night. Inside the cast-iron grilles of the park cannas and geraniums bloomed, two fountains spurted jets of water which fell tinkling into iron basins, the freshly cut lawns smelt sweet and warm. Northwards, over the elms bordering the pavement, rose the tip of St Jude's tower with its lighted clock dial round and bright and yellow as a harvest moon, across from it an ancient Quaker meeting house stood demurely in its small graveyard, and round the plaza ancient mansions, red-brick, white-marble trimmed, stood like old veterans in a hollow square. For the most part they had been made into 'maisonettes' for people in the upper-middle-income tax brackets, but outwardly they retained the air of hauteur they had worn when Oakey Hall was mayor and Boss Tweed a scandal in New York politics. The July moon hung low in the sky, a disc of scorched gold with the branches of the elms and sycamores on its face as if drawn with charcoal, and every park bench held its complement of lovers. Lovers strolled along the cement paths, each pair absorbed in themselves as if they had been the last people in the world; the tarnished moonlight was a mellow wonderland to them.

Angela caught her breath with a small sad sound that was not quite a sob, but something not far from it. She had been a young wife, almost a bride, when Darcy died, but she had found some measure of solace in the knowledge that beneath her heart she bore that which would give him immortality;

'To die would not be dying quite,
Leaving a little life behind. . . .'

And since she had been born with the proverbial silver spoon in her mouth she reared Darcy's son in a mellow atmosphere of ancestors, heirlooms and family tradition. All that came to him by nature had a chance to grow and develop and the final product was a slim brown man with curling hair and a quick friendly smile for whom the title 'gentleman' seemed to have been hand-tailored and to whom clung the faint fragrance of gentle living.

She loved him for his sweet and winsome self, but more than that she loved him as his father's surrogate. In him the high hopes she and Darcy had dreamed in their short ecstasy of marriage were to be fulfilled, he would perpetuate the Logan name; born in a world cleansed of the curse of war by countless bloody sacrifices of his father's generation he would achieve the thing that fate denied his father. Already he had shown a more than merely casual interest in the daughter of one of her classmates, and she had dreamed of being a grandmother before time had stolen strength and beauty from her.

Then December 7th, 1941, the blare of trumpets and the roll of drums and streets resounding to the pound of marching feet. Training camp . . . letters from England . . . the Normandy invasion . . . 'the War Department regrets . . .'.

There were tears in her heart that would not come to her eyes for relief as she heard a girl's low 'Always?' and her lover's promised 'Always and for ever, dear,' as a young couple passed her.

'There,' a shrill vindictive voice seemed whispering, 'there but for some drop stitch of Fate go Harold and Geraldine.' All at once she felt unutterably old. Old and tired. Her hands felt numb and in the hollows of her shoulders ached a fine pain. 'Oh, Harold, my poor, sweet boy,' she murmured hopelessly. Blinded with sudden tears, almost all life gone from her fine, pliant body, lost and forsaken as a derelict, she leaned against the park's iron fence, sobbing with short retching sobs like the breathing of a spent runner.

Mr Chips strained at the leash, shrank fearfully into the shadow of a friendly tree, dropped upon his stomach with a terrified whimper. The pull upon the lead roused her, and she straightened, then stepped back with a short involuntary 'Oh!'

Within arm's length of her stood a small neat gentleman in black mohair with a Panama hat set jauntily on one side of his head and a gold-headed black malacca stick swung jauntily from his hand. His dark, lined face and short white beard and moustache were those of an old man but his bearing was decidedly sprightly and his eyes very bright. They were unusual eyes, dark but not black, with little flecks of garnet in them.

They seemed to have no division between the irises and pupils and their habitual expression was one of heavy-lidded weariness, as though they had looked too closely at life for a long time. Just then, however, they were bent on her with a look of dispassionate irony which seemed more curious than malicious.

'You are in trouble, Madame?' He spoke with the slightest of slight accents, in the almost colourless tone of the perfect linguist. There was a suave, foreign-bred something in his words and manner, and the gesture with which he doffed his wide hat was somehow reminiscent of a Versailles courtier in the days when Bourbons sat upon the throne of France.

Angela gave back a step. Without quite knowing why she was afraid of this small harmless-looking gentleman with courtly manners, but the fear was natural and intuitive as that felt when one gazes into a snake-pit at the zoo. 'There's nothing anyone can do to help,' she answered shortly, tightened her hold on the dog's leash and stepped towards the curb to pass the little man.

'One moment, if you please.' His voice, still soft, was mandatory in its even tone. 'You are in trouble, yet you say no one can help you. Are you sure?'

She braced herself as for a physical assault. Instinctively she knew something was coming, something which might change the whole rhythm of life. She took a short breath, let it out soundlessly, then, 'Of course, I'm sure.' Her tone was razor-sharp with finality.

'There you make a mistake, Madame,' the suave reply was compelling in its monotone. 'There is nothing – understand me, *nothing* – which we cannot have if we desire it enough and are willing to pay its price.'

'Pay?' her voice rose almost to a scream. 'Dear God, I'd pay anything –'

'Anything, Madame –' There was irony, perhaps a hint of malice in the echoed word.

'Anything!'

'Then listen carefully, Madame.' He fumbled in the pocket of his jacket and brought out a little doll-like image scarcely longer than her thumb. 'Take this for a talisman. Concentrate your thought – your wish – on it. If you are strong enough in your desire – and if you do not haggle at the price – you may attain your wish, though whether it will bring you happiness or not I should not care to say.'

Mechanically her fingers closed round the little puppet, and as she thanked him with an inclination of her head the little gentleman added, 'If you should need me again throw the charm away and call me.'

Despite herself Angela laughed. 'How can I call you? I don't even know your name.'

'You will know what name to call if the need comes, Madame.' The little man made her another bow which would have been a credit to a dancing master at the court of Louis XV. Then he replaced his hat at its slightly rakish angle and swinging his black cane strode off into the shadows.

Three times Angela made a gesture of casting the doll into the gutter as she walked back to her house, but each time, smiling mirthlessly at herself for her weakness, she refrained. Back in her drawing-room she snapped on the desk light and examined it.

It was carved or moulded of some hard substance, perhaps soap-stone or pottery, which had a velvety smoothness and retained an almost reptilian coolness despite the heat of the night and the warmth of her hand. The maker had shaped it to represent a man, or the grotesque of one, dressed in a medieval costume which consisted of long, pointed shoes, tight hose bound round with cross-garters, a loosely-hanging gabardine or cloak with foliated edges and sleeve-openings, and a close-fitting hood upon the head through which two openings had been cut to leave the ears exposed. The figure made her think of Punchinello, wide-shouldered, hunchbacked, with exaggeratedly sharp nose and chin, thick beetling brows above pop eyes, and a malicious, mocking grin. Somehow there was an air of hatefulness about it, an intimation of malevolence and animosity that repelled and yet fascinated her. The more she looked at it the more repulsive it seemed, and yet it had a certain charm like that which English bulldogs have by virtue of their very ugliness.

'He was an absurd little man,' she told herself, 'with all his foreign airs and graces, and his awful deadly earnestness. . . .' Her voice trailed off, became mute, for another thought had crowded into her brain. 'Use this as a talisman,' he had said, 'and concentrate your thought on it. If you are strong enough in your desire. . . .'

She rose, hands knotted into fists, and gazed at the small statuette. Her eyes were fixed, intense, half-closed, as if the violence of her gaze were too annihilating to be loosed direct; as if the substance of her soul and body would pour out of her set, staring orbs. 'My boy,' she whispered in a voice so low as to be hardly audible, but harsh as an abrasive scraped across metal. 'Give back my son – put back the universe and give us yesterday!'

Somewhere in the distance thunder rattled with a crackle like the sound of far-off musketry, into the heavy, humid air there crept a chill as tangible as smoke, and the sky shattered with a dazzling burst of yellow-green lightning.

She flinched from the flash as the telephone began ringing, at first querulously, then frantically, drilling at her, 'Hello?' she greeted somewhat shakily, still startled by the lightning.

'Mother?' Her stomach suddenly felt stiff and empty, she could not fight down the weakness that chilled her with pulse-stopping cold. Weak-kneed as a rag doll from which the stuffing has been ripped, she dropped into a chair. What line, if any, divides sanity from madness, where does sanity end and madness begin? she wondered. Was this a trick of overwrought senses and gnawing desire, or was she the victim of an unspeakably cruel hoax?

'Who – who is this?' she contrived at last, and in the little interval of silence she could hear the pounding of her heart like a jazz-drummer's rataplan.

'Whom do you think?'

Another silence, one that hummed electrically. Then: 'This joke's not in the best of taste,' her voice was hard and gritty.

'Oh, *maman*, you'll be what the Heinies couldn't – the death o' me!' It was the well-remembered laugh that stirred her pulses like a long note on a trumpet.

'But – but – you're – you were –'

'No, I'm not, I assure you. Officially or not, I'm still alive and likely to be kickin' if you don't snap out of it. The report of my death was greatly exaggerated, old dear. I did have a tough time, and spent a tour of duty in hospital *sans* memory, *sans* dog-tags, *sans* everything but life. But here I am like the proverbial bad penny, safe and moderately sound. Be with you in a little while – just landed at the airport.'

She was radiantly, arrogantly happy. Like one who wakens from a long dream-haunted night to find a morning with cool, limpid air and sunlight sparkling over everything. The twitterings of sparrow in the park seemed like a canticle: *For this my son was dead and is alive again; he was lost and is found.* Her face was transfigured by happiness as by a halo. The sunshine had a brighter gold, even when it rained the drops fell brightly, gleaming, jewel-like, on the trees and window panes.

At first she did not notice the small, subtle changes in him, the absence of the little niceties which had been as inherent as his breath. When he did not hold her chair at dinner or rise when she came into the room she overlooked it. War was dirty, dull, dangerous and degrading, small wonder it had rasped the patina of refinement from him. He had been meticulously neat, physically and mentally, now he was slovenly about his room, with clothes left carelessly on floor or chair or bed; in place of his alert, attentive manner he seemed oddly distraught. He would sit for minutes staring endlessly at nothing, his eyes strange, far-away, almost filmy with ennui, his shoulders slumping, as if nothing really mattered. Small blame to him, she thought. He had been to the very gates of hell; could she expect him to come back unmarked?

Even when he showed no interest in employment she made excuses. A man who had had death for a bedfellow and boon companion could hardly be expected to take interest in a desk job, or grow enthusiastic over selling things. No matter, she had plenty for them both.

But had she? When he asked her for five hundred dollars for 'a deal' she was delighted. He had determined to launch out for himself, not take an underling's position. When the deal fell through and he asked for a thousand she was more puzzled than worried. She had neither aptitude for nor experience in business, and knew only that men made or lost money in it. Harold, it appeared, was one of those who lost, for in a month he needed more, then more. Her income was derived from funds invested by the trust department of her bank, and earnings had not been as great this year as last. One morning came a notice from the bank that she was overdrawn. She made the necessary arrangements, sold off some bonds, and – had another notice of an overdraft within six weeks.

She knew she had not drawn five thousand dollars in one cheque, and went down to the bank to see about it. There it was, payable to Harold Logan, made out in her own handwriting, signed with her own signature. But the signature was not hers.

'Oh, yes, now I remember,' she told the cashier, and embarrassment brought a quick flush to her face. 'I had forgotten – this.'

The complete absence of expression in the banker's face voiced scepticism sharper than his words. 'That's your signature, Mrs Logan?'

'Why, yes, of course,' she spoke with more than necessary emphasis. 'Of course, it's mine. Why do you ask?'

'Our teller was a little doubtful, but the cheque's entirely in your writing, and the payee is your son –'

L

'I don't think you need make yourselves uneasy over any cheque my son presents.' She spaced her syllables precisely, so they sounded clipped and hard.

The visitor was not the sort of person she was used to entertaining. He was something less than middle height, dark-skinned, black-haired, curly-haired. His light grey, almost white suit had been pressed into knife-sharp creases, from the breast pocket of his jacket spilled a grey-silk handker-chief, he had been freshly shaved and manicured and exuded a faint odour of brandy, garlic and lilac perfume. His brown skin shone as if it had been rubbed with oil, his eyes danced with a light more sinister than merry, his full, too-red lips framed a smile more nearly contemptuous than good-humoured.

He did not, however, lack directions. 'You're Logan's old lady?' he asked.

'I am Mrs Logan.'

'Uh-huh.' He looked at her, a little puzzled, just a little uneasy. His eyes swept up and down her as if they had been adding a column of figures and were not entirely satisfied with the answer. At last: 'You love 'im, don't you?'

'I'm sure you didn't call to ascertain the strength of my maternal affection, Mr –' she paused interrogatively, and the cold, slightly amused contempt of her gaze seared him as an early frost withers a row of larkspur.

'Huh? Oh –' He fumbled for a word, then brought his reply out, and with it an oblong of green paper. 'I'll tell th' cockeyed world I didn't. I come here to get gelt for this.' He held the slip out, a cheque made payable to Joseph Lanzilotti in the sum of seven hundred dollars, signed with her name.

'I don't remember making any cheque to you, Mr Lanzilotti.'

'Don't, huh? Then it's just too bad for your kid. That's all I gotta say.'

'I don't think I quite understand –'

'Lemme fill you in, lady. He rolled me Saturday night in a crap game, your kid, that is, an' when I took 'im for a half gran' he give me this IOU. Nex' day he come and gimme this' – he indicated the cheque – 'an' got two hun'nert fish in change for it. See? Then when I goes to th' bank this mornin' they reneges on th' signature. Says they gotta have your OK 'fore they'll lemme have th' money. Come clean, lady. Slap your OK on it, or little Harold goes to th' pokey. See?'

'You make it very clear, Mr Lanzilotti.' She took the cheque, endorsed it, 'OK. Angela Logan,' and returned it. 'In future I'd advise you not to play games with my son,' she cautioned as she went with him to the door. 'I might not see your point so readily next time.'

Joe Lanzilotti knew when he was outclassed. Also, from long frequenting of race courses, he knew a thoroughbred when he saw one. 'Sure, lady,' he agreed as he tipped his pearl-grey Homburg with more than customary flourish, 'I won't never let th' bum come in my jernt ag'in, an' I'll top all th' other mugs to give 'im th' shoo-fly if he comes buzzin' round th' gallopin' dominoes.'

She had just the sort of dinner that delighted him that night, steak two inches thick, the tenderloin charred on the outside, pink as a poodle's tongue inside, lyonnaise potatoes, chicory salad and a chocolate pie. Since he no longer cared for sherry as an aperitif she chilled a shaker of Manhattans and had a bottle of Nuits St Georges brought up from the cellar. But when he came in so late, the steak was ruined and the cocktails little more than ice water, he was slightly tipsy and more than a little truculent. 'Got here soon as I could,' he explained rather than apologized. 'That dam' subway –'

She noted that he made no move to kiss her, and was stung by the omission. 'Oh, that's all right, son. If you can stand cold steak I'm sure the steak and I don't mind waiting –'

'Good Lord, steak again? I swear to God I'm getting so I daren't look a cow in the eye –' His nonchalance was poorly worn as he dropped into his chair.

She filled their glasses, tasted hers, then stared silently into its ruddy depths. 'A friend of yours was here today, Harold. A Mr Lanzilotti – quite a character.'

'Eh?' She saw his eyes go suddenly wide, startled and questioning, a little frightened. 'What'd he want?'

'You ought to know –'

His chair crashed on the floor as he rose, glaring at her. 'Well, what're you going to do? Send me up for forgery –'

'Harold!'

'All right, you needn't be dramatic about it.' There was a morose recklessness about his pose as he stalked from the room, but at the doorway he came to a halt and in the courtly way he bowed his head before he left there was an echo of the old, aristocratic elegance that marked his every move in former days.

She lit a cigarette, stubbed out its fire before it had a chance to glow, then lit another. In her heart there was a dull ache and her knees felt weak and unsubstantial. She wasn't sure she could stand. Any moment, she knew, she might be sick.

The shrilling of the doorbell wakened her from her trancelike misery, and the tap-tap of high heels that followed was like a tonic. Geraldine Macfarland! Mightn't Gerry be the answer to her problem? Harold had been more than casually interested in her before he went away; she'd done everything she could to throw them together since his return. Angela was only nineteen years older than her son, but they were of different generations, just the same. She was not one of those fatuous fools who boasted she and her offspring were 'pals', but Gerry – perhaps romantic love could work a reformation where maternal affection failed.

'Gerry, dear,' she greeted, holding out slim bare arms to the girl, 'I'm so glad you – why, what's the matter, darling?'

Gerry's pretty pink-and-white face was ravaged as a garden following a savage storm, and the hands that seized hers were cold while the cheek that pressed against hers burned as if with fever. 'Aunt Angela,' the passionless, cold little voice went into her like a dentist's drill, 'I've got to talk to you – and Harold – right away.'

'Of course,' she led the way to the drawing-room and dropped down on a love seat, pulling the girl down beside her. 'Now, what is it, dear?'

Gerry's slender fingers wreathed and unwreathed, twisting blindly, futilely as worms. 'It's about Harold – me – us, Aunt Angela. I've been feeling miserable for some time, nauseated nearly every morning, nervous as a cat, pains in my chest. Today I called on Dr Christy. He says I'm – we're – going to have –'

The world seemed suddenly to have stopped, and breathing with it. The silence was so overpowering Angela could hear the blood pound in her throat. Then, like a gallant boxer, beaten, but determined to fight to the final knockout, she rallied. '*Autres temps, autres moeurs,* dear,' somehow she contrived a smile which was a reasonable facsimile of the real thing. 'In my day this would have been a scandal, but you and Harold can be married quietly –'

'That's just it! He won't –'

'Oh, *no-o*!' Stark, utter misery made her voice quaver. 'He couldn't be such a cad. Not –'

His footsteps slightly unsteady, came down the stairs. He was humming:

> *'The minstrels sing of a jovial king;*
> *A wonderful king was he. . . .'*

He halted at the doorway. 'Goin' out, Mom. Goin' to give the gals a treat – Hi, Gerry,' he waved an indifferent greeting to the caller. 'Be seein' you around sometime –'

'Harold!' How she kept her voice from breaking, kept from screaming, Angela had no idea. 'Come here – sit down – I want to talk –'

'Eh?' He shot a sharp glance from her to the girl. 'Oh, I see, she's told you –'

'Yes, she's told me –'

'And just what are you goin' to do about it?'

'I think that you're the one to answer that.'

'Do, eh? Well, I can answer in one word; Nothing. How does she know that it was I – how do I know –'

'Oh, Harold!' Geraldine's voice was pitched shrill, but controlled. 'Oh, how could you – and I loved you so!'

He laughed, and Angela felt everything inside her shrivel as if touched with live flame.

This was no laugh of bravado, no brazen attempt to face indecency. He was amused – that was the devilish, unbelievable thing about it.

She had risen to face him, now she took a step back. Her lips opened, then shut again. With apocalyptic clarity she saw him as if for the first time. She could look through him distinctly as if using a spiritual X-ray. And he was bad. Rotten clear through as maggot-bitten fruit is rotten.

Raw misery was stark in her eyes as they swept round the room and came to momentary rest upon the figurine the little foreign gentleman had given her the night Harold came home. 'Saint Punchinello,' she had called the thing affectionately, the patron who had brought her dead back to her. Now her gaze hardened, froze like water into a sudden zero temperature. In three quick, almost stumbling steps she crossed the room and snatched the statuette from the desk. Something deep inside herself – or perhaps a thing outside – put the words she had never heard before in her mouth,

'*Barran-Sathanas!*' she called in a voice that was like a dissonant chord. '*Barran-Sathanas!*' She hurled the image from her as if it had been a loathsome reptile.

Outside the November night was still as ice and bitter cold, the moonlight struck chill fire from frost-encrusted paving stones, the stars shone with a crystalline brightness, and not a cloud showed in the smalt-blue sky, but as the little figure struck the base-board and shattered as if it had been blown glass there came a distant cannonade of thunder and a zigzag lance of lightning slashed through the sky like a sword through flesh. The front door – she knew that it was latched and chained! – swung open and a step sounded in the hall.

'*Eh bien*, Madame,' said the small gentleman as he bowed in the doorway leading from the hall to the drawing-room, 'it seems you have repented of your bargain. You find the price too high?'

He wore a faultless dinner kit, black pearls glowed dully in his shirtfront, the thick white hair that sloped up from a widow's peak on his forehead was brushed back sleekly in a pompadour, his little white moustache and beard were neatness personified, but there was that in his lined face that bludgeoned her with horror. His features were not so much old as ancient, yet they seemed ageless too; he seemed to be a part of that which had been, was, and was to be.

Somehow she found her voice, forced throat and tongue and lips to function. 'The price?' she echoed, and her whisper was a queer small ghost of sound, 'Dear God, yes, it's too high! I would not call my boy – my fine, clean, gentle boy – back from his honoured grave to be a thing like this. I would not slake the thirst of my sorrow if quenching it means misery to Geraldine –'

'Your sentiments do you great credit, Madame, but should you not have thought of all that when you asked that the universe be turned back?'

'How could I know. . .?'

'True, Madame, how could you? But you were warned the price might be exorbitant –'

'Take me!' she broke in between chattering teeth. 'Kill my body, rend it, tear it – burn my wretched soul for all eternity in your hell, but put my dear, brave son back where he belongs with the honoured dead who died for decency and freedom. Let him lie in the earth hallowed by his blood, and by the blood of other mothers' sons –'

'Your soul, Madame?' He brushed his wisp of white moustache with the knuckle of a bent forefinger. 'You put extraordinary value on a bit of rather trumpery *bijouterie*, don't you? Besides, what need have I for more souls? From Rome, Berlin and Tokyo, from Moscow and Madrid –?' He waved a deprecating hand. 'Really, I suffer an embarrassment of riches. Sometimes I think I'll have to set a quota on the importations.'

She dropped to her knees, inched towards him, held up empty, supplicating hands. 'Barran – great Barran-Sathanas – Lord and Master –'

'Don't be a fool,' he said as casually as if refusing a second cup of coffee.

'Take me, take me, mighty Lord of the World, do with me as you will, only give my boy back to the earth made sacred by his blood –'

'You annoy me, Madame. Once every thousand years or so it pleases me to strike a bargain, then remit the *quid pro quo*. Think well; there is no turning back this time. You would not have your son restored to life; you are willing that he go down to the grave again –'

'I beg you, I beseech you; I entreat you –'

'So be it. Have it as you wish.' His sharp eyes bored into hers, and in them the small garnet speckings seemed to glow to incandescence. 'Have your wish, mother. And this' – he bent above her, laid two fingers on her bowed head – 'this is for remembering.'

Only once before had Angela felt anything like it. That was when as a child she had held the electrodes of a galvanic battery while a playmate ground the generator. Every nerve seemed suddenly knotted, all her muscles twisted into ropes of pain, a light as dazzling as aurora borealis flared before her eyes, her throat closed in quick, agonizing contraction, her breath stopped and she wilted to the floor with no more life in her than a dead thing.

Slowly consciousness returned. The big room echoed small sounds hollowly, like an empty auditorium. Outside she heard the splashing of the fountains and the distant gleeful shouts of children romping under street-showers. Somewhere not far away two cats indulging in illicit romance split the air with feline love calls and the big clock in the hall ticked with deliberate decorum. A little breeze stirred the curtains at the front windows, and over all was the soft, clinging sultriness of a July night.

She sat up, pressed the back of her hand to her forehead a bewildered moment, and got slowly to her feet. 'I dreamed it,' she told herself tremulously. 'How horrible!' Yet had it been only a dream? In olden days the Lord spoke to Jacob and Samuel, giving them a vision past their waking senses. Might she not have been vouchsafed such a boon? If Harold had come back and – 'Dear Lord, I thank Thee for this mercy,' she murmured. 'He's safe where he is, safe always and for ever, secure in honoured glory –'

She tottered to the desk, took up the Army form, wrote acceptance of the first option in a firm hand. Let the young oak lie where it had fallen; let him lie beside his comrades with his white cross above him, and over all, triumphantly, the flag he died to serve. . . . Some little spot of earth that is for ever home. . . .

She glanced up. In the glass above the desk she saw her reflection. Across the dark hair waved above her forehead was a double line of startling white, as if two fingers lightly dipped in flour had been laid on it.

EVAN HUNTER

The Korean War brought psychological treatment (or brain-washing) of prisoners of war to the notice of the general public although the technique had been used in the Second World War. The special conditions which existed in the battle areas of Korea reduced soldiers quickly to a state of battle fatigue and this made it possible for psychological treatment to be applied to prisoners without the necessity of a long period of 'conditioning' to break down their resistance to suggestion.

Battle fatigue produces a mental state of disorientation, unreality and fantasy and it was from this basis that Evan Hunter produced this, perhaps inevitable, tale of a demented soldier. When, at the very breaking point, the soldier in *The Scarlet King* defeated his enemy the battle within his mind was just beginning.

12 · THE SCARLET KING

IT was the little things that annoyed him, always the little things, those and of course the king of hearts.

If only these little things didn't bother him so, if only he could look at them dispassionately and say, 'You don't bother me, you *can't* bother me,' everything would be all right. But that wasn't the way it worked. They did bother him. They started by gnawing at his nerves, tiny little nibbles of annoyance until his nerves were frayed and ready to unravel. And then the restless annoyance spread to his muscles, until his face began to tic and his hands began to clench and unclench spasmodically. He could not control the tic or the unconscious spasms of his hands, and his inability to control them annoyed him even more until he was filled with a futile sort of frustrated rage, and it was always then that the king of hearts popped into his mind.

Even now, even just thinking about the things that annoyed him, he could see the king. It was not a one-eyed king like the king of diamonds, oh no. The king of hearts had two eyes, two eyes that stared up from the cynically sneering face on the card. The king held a sword in his hand, but the sword was hidden, oh so cleverly hidden, held aloft ready to strike, but only the hilt and a very small portion of the blade was visible, and the rest of the sword, the part that could tear and hack and rip, was hidden behind the king's head and crown.

He was a clever king, the king of hearts, and he was the cause of everything, of why the annoyances got out of hand occasionally, he was the cause, all right, he was the cause, that two-eyed clever louse, *why doesn't that girl upstairs stop playing that god-damned piano*!

Now just a minute, he told himself. Just get a grip, because if you don't get a grip, we're going to be in trouble. Now just forget that little rat is up there pounding those scales, up and down, up and down, *do, re, mi, fa, so, la, ti, do, ti, la, so.* . . .

Forget her!

Dammit, forget her!

159

He crossed the room, and slammed down the window, but he could still hear the monotonous sound of the little girl at the piano upstairs, a sound which seeped through the floorboards and dripped down the walls. He covered his ears with his cupped palms, but the sound leaked through his fingers, *do, re, mi, fa, so. . . .*

Think of something else, he commanded himself.

Think of Tom.

It was very nice of Tom to have loaned him the apartment. Tom was a good brother, one of the best. And it was very nice of him to have parted with the apartment so willingly, but of course he'd been going on a hunting trip anyway, so the apartment would be empty all week-end, and Tom couldn't possibly have known about the girl upstairs and her goddamned piano. Tom knew that things were annoying him a lot, but he didn't know the half of it, God he'd turn purple if he knew the half of it, but even so he couldn't be blamed for that monotonous little girl upstairs.

He had seen the girl yesterday, walking with her mother in the little park across the street, a nice-looking little girl, and a pretty mother, and he smiled and nodded his head, but that was before he knew the little girl was an aspiring impressario. Today, he had seen the mother leaving shortly before noon, heading across the park with the autumn wind lapping at her skirts. And shortly after that, the piano had started.

It was close to two o'clock now, and the mother still hadn't returned, and the piano had gone since noon, up and down those damn scales, when would she stop, wouldn't she ever stop practising, how long does someone have to practise in order to. . . ?

We're back on that again, he thought, and that's dangerous. We have to forget the little annoyances because he just loves these little annoyances. When the annoyances get out of hand, he steps in with his leering face and the sword hidden behind his crown, so we can't let the annoyances get out of hand. So she's practising a piano, what's so terrible about that? Isn't a little girl allowed to practise a piano? Isn't this a free country? Goddammit, didn't I fight to keep it free?

He didn't want to think about the fighting, either, but he had thought about it, and now it was full-blown in his mind, and he knew he could not shove it out of his mind until he had examined every facet of the living nightmare that had been with him since that day.

It had been a clear day, the weather in Korea surprisingly like the

weather in New York, and it had been quiet all along the front, and everyone was talking about this being it, this being the end. He hadn't known whether or not to believe the rumours, but it had certainly felt like the end, not even a rifle shot since early the night before, the entire front as still and as complacent as a mountain lake.

He had sat in the foxhole with Scarpa, a New York boy he had known since his days at Fort Dix. They had played cut-throat poker all morning, and Scarpa had won heavily, pulling in the matchsticks which served as poker chips, each matchstick representing a dollar note. They had taken a break for food, and then they'd gone back to the game, and Scarpa kept winning, winning heavily, and Scarpa's good luck began to annoy him. He had lifted each newly dealt hand with a sort of desperate urgency, wanting to beat Scarpa now, wanting desperately to win. When Scarpa dealt him the ten, jack, queen, and ace of hearts, he had reached for his fifth card eagerly, hoping it was the king, hoping he could sit there smugly with a royal flush while Scarpa confidently bet into him.

The fifth card had been a four of clubs.

He was surprised to find his hands trembling. He looked across the mess kit that served as a table, and he discarded the four of clubs and said, 'One card.'

Scarpa looked up at him curiously.

'Two pair?' he asked, a slight smile on his face.

'Just give me one card, that's all.'

'Sure,' Scarpa said.

He dealt the card face down on the mess kit.

'I'm pat,' Scarpa said, smiling.

He reached for the card. If Scarpa was pat, he was holding either a straight, a flush, or a full house. Or maybe he just had two pair and hadn't drawn for fear he'd give away his hand. That was not likely, though. If Scarpa thought he was playing against a man who already held two pair, he'd have taken a card, hoping to fill in one of the pair.

No, Scarpa was sitting with a straight, a flush, or a full house.

If he drew the king of hearts, he would beat Scarpa.

'Bet five bucks,' Scarpa said.

He still did not pick up the face-down card. He threw ten matchsticks into the pot and said, 'Raise you five.'

'Without looking at your cards?' Scarpa asked incredulously.

'I'm raising five. Are you in this, or not?'

Scarpa smirked. 'Sure. And since we're playing big time, let's kick it up another ten.'

He looked across at Scarpa. He knew he should pick up the card and look at it, but there was something about Scarpa's insolent attitude that goaded him. He did not pick up the card.

'Let's put it all on this hand,' he said bravely. 'All that I owe you. Double or nothing.'

'Without picking up that card?' Scarpa asked.

'Yes.'

'You can't beat me without that fifth card. You know that, don't you?'

'Double or nothing, I said.'

Scarpa shrugged. 'Sure. Double or nothing. It's a deal. Pick up your card.'

'Maybe I don't need the card,' he said. 'Maybe I'm sitting here with four of a kind.'

Scarpa chuckled. 'Maybe,' he said. 'But it better be a *high* four of a kind.'

He felt his first twinge of panic then. He had figured Scarpa wrong. Scarpa was probably holding a low four of a kind, which meant he *had* to fill the royal flush now. A high straight wouldn't do the trick. It had to be the king of hearts.

He reached for the card, and lifted it.

He felt first a wild exultance, a sweeping sort of triumph that lashed at his body when he saw the king with his upraised, partially hidden sword. He lifted his head and opened his mouth, ready to shout, 'A royal flush!' and then he saw the Mongol.

The Mongol was a big man, and he held a bigger sword, and for a moment he couldn't believe that what he was seeing was real. He looked back to the king of hearts, and he opened his mouth wide to shriek a warning to Scarpa, but the Mongol was lifting his sword, the biggest sword he'd ever seen in his life, and then the sword came down in a sweeping, glittering arc, and he saw pain register on Scarpa's face when the blade struck, and then his head parted in the centre, like an apple under a sharp paring knife, and the blood squirted out of his eyes and his nose and his mouth.

He looked at Scarpa, and then he looked again at the Mongol, and he thought only *I had a royal flush, I had a royal flush.* He found his bayonet in his hand. He saw his arm swinging back, and then he hacked downward at the Mongol, and he saw the stripe of red appear on the side of the Mongol's neck, and he struck again, and again, until the Mongol's neck and shoulder was a gushing red tangle of ribbons. The Mongol collapsed into the foxhole, the length of him falling over the scattered cards. Alongside his body, the king of hearts smirked.

The CO couldn't understand how the Mongol had got through the lines. He reprimanded his men, and then he noticed the strange dazed expression on the face of the man who'd slain the Mongol. He sent him to the field hospital at once.

The medics called it shock, and they worked over him, and finally they made sense out of his gibberish, but not enough sense. They shipped him back to the States. The bug doctors talked to him, and they gave him occupational therapy, mystified when he refused to play cards with the other men. They had seen men affected by killing before. Not all men could kill. A man who could not kill was worthless to the Army. They discharged him.

They had not known it was all because of that royal flush. They had not known how annoyed he'd been with Scarpa all that day, and how that red king of hearts, that scarlet king, was the key to unravelling all that annoyance.

Now, in the safety of his brother's apartment, he thought of that day again, and he thought of the Mongol's intrusion, and of how his triumph had been shattered by that intrusion. If only it had been different. If only he could have said, 'I have a royal flush, Scarpa, you louse. Look at it! Look at it, and let me see that goddamned smirk vanish! Look at it, Scarpa!'

The Mongol had divided the smirk on Scarpa's face, but the king of hearts had lain there in the bottom of the foxhole, and nothing erased that superior smirk on his face, nothing, nothing.

It was bad. He knew that it was bad. You're not supposed to react this way. Normal people don't react this way. If a little girl is playing the piano, you let her play. *God, when is she going to stop!*

You don't start getting annoyed, not if you're normal. You don't let these things bother you until you can't control them any more.

Tom wouldn't let these little things annoy him. Tom was all right, and hadn't Tom been through a war? The big war, not the child's play in

Korea, but had Tom ever seen a Mongol cavalry attack, with gongs sounding, and trumpets blaring, had Tom ever seen that, ever experienced the horrible stench of fear when you stood in the path of the advancing horses?

Well, the Mongol he'd killed hadn't been on horseback, so he couldn't use that as an excuse. The Mongol was, in a way, a very vulnerable man, despite his hugeness and the size of his sword. The bayonet had split his skin just like any man's, and his blood had flown as red as the woman's in Baltimore.

I don't want to think about the woman in Baltimore, he told himself.

He looked up at the ceiling of the room, and he prayed *Please, little girl, please stop playing the piano. Please, please.*

Do, re, mi, fa, so, la, ti. . . .

The woman in Baltimore had been a nice old lady. Except for the way she smacked her lips. He had lived in the room across the hall from her, and she'd always invited him in for tea in the afternoon, and she'd served those very nice little cookies with chocolate trails of icing across their tops. He had liked the cookies and the tea, until he'd begun noticing the way the old lady smacked her lips. She had very withered, parched lips, and every time she sipped at her tea, she smacked them with a loud purse, and there was something disgusting about it, something almost obscene. It began to annoy him.

It began to annoy him the way Scarpa had annoyed him that day in the foxhole.

He tried to stay away from the old lady, but he couldn't. He wanted to go in there and say, 'Can't you stop that goddamn vulgar smacking of your lips, you sanctimonious old hag?' That would have shut her up, all right. That would have shown her he wasn't going to take any more of her disgusting slurping.

But he could not bring himself to do it, and so she continued to annoy him, until his face began to tic, and his hands began to tremble, and one day he seized a knife from her kitchen drawer and hacked at her neck, until her jugular vein split in a scarlet bubble of blood.

He had left Baltimore.

He had gone down to Miami and taken a job as a beach boy in one of the big hotels. He had always been a good swimmer, a man who should have been put in underwater demolition or something, not dumped into a

M

foxhole with people who couldn't swim at all. He had been lucky in Baltimore because the old lady herself ran the boarding house in which he'd stayed. There was one other boarder, an old man who never left his room. The old lady was the only person who'd known his name, and she wasn't telling it to anyone, not any more.

But in Miami, faced with what he had done, afraid it might happen again, he took on an assumed name, a name he had forgotten now. Everyone called him by his assumed name, and he garnered fat tips from the sun-tanned people who lolled at the edge of the swimming pool. And all he'd had to do was arrange their beach chairs or get them a drink of orange juice every now and then. It was a good life, and he felt very warm and very healthy, and he thought for a while that he would forget all about the king of hearts and the Mongol and the old lady in Baltimore.

Until Carl began getting wise.

He hadn't liked Carl to begin with. Carl was one of these sinewy muscular guys who always put on a big show at the diving board, one of those characters who liked to swim the length of the pool six times underwater, and then brag about it later.

Carl's bragging began to get on his nerves. All right, Carl *was* a good swimmer, but he was good too!

It started one night while they were vacuuming out the bottom of the pool.

'I'm wasting my time in this dump,' Carl said. 'I should be working in a water show someplace.'

'You're not that good,' he'd answered.

Carl looked up. 'What do you mean by that?'

'Just what I said. I've seen better swimmers.'

'You have, huh?'

'Yes, I have.'

'Who, for instance? Johnny Weissmuller?'

'No, I wasn't talking about Johnny Weissmuller. I've just seen better swimmers, that's all. Even I can swim better than you.'

'You think so, huh?'

'Yes, I think so. In fact, I know so. I won a PAL medal when I was a kid. For swimming.'

'You know what you can do with a PAL medal, don't you?' Carl asked.

'I'm only saying it because I want you to know you're not so hot, that's all.'

'Kid, maybe you'd like to put your money where your mouth is, huh?'

'How do you mean?'

'A contest. Any stroke you call, or all of the strokes, if you like. We'll race across the pool. What do you say?'

'Any time,' he answered.

'How much have you got to lose?'

'I'll bet you everything I've saved since I've been here.'

'And how much is that?'

'About five hundred bucks.'

'It's a bet,' Carl said, and he extended his hand and sealed the bargain.

The bet disturbed him. Now that he had made it, he was not at all sure he *could* swim better than Carl, not at all sure. He thought about it, and the more he thought about it, the more annoyed he became, until finally the familiar tic and trembling broke out again, and he felt this frustrated rage within him. He wanted to call off the bet, tell Carl he'd seen better swimmers and even *he* was a better swimmer, but he saw no reason to have to prove it, so what the hell, why should he waste his time for a measly five hundred bucks? That's what he wanted to tell Carl, but he realized that would sound like chickening out, and he didn't know what to do, and his annoyance mounted, and back of it all was that scarlet king, and he hated that card with all his might, and his hatred spread to include Carl.

He could not go through with the match.

He stole a bread knife from the kitchen on the night before he was to swim, and he went to Carl's room. Carl was surprised to see him, and he was even more surprised when the knife began hacking at his neck and shoulder in even regular strokes until he collapsed lifeless and blood-spattered to the floor.

It was all because of the king of hearts. All because of that clever, sneaky character with the hidden sword.

The petrol station attendant in Georgia, on the way up North, that had been the worst, because that man had annoyed him only a very little bit, haggling over the price of the petrol, but he had hit him anyway, hit him with the sharp cleaving edge of a tyre iron, knocked him flat to the concrete of his one-man filling station, and then hacked away at him until the man was unrecognizable.

And now, the little girl upstairs, pounding the piano, annoying him in the same way all the others had annoyed him, annoying, annoying until he would see red, and in that red, the king would take shape, leering.

If he could defeat the king, of course, he could defeat all the rest of them.

It was just a matter of looking the king straight in the eye, even when he was being terribly annoyed, looking him straight in the eye, and not allowing him to take hold. Why, of course, that was the ticket! What was he, anyway? Just a card, wasn't he? Couldn't he stare down a card? What was so difficult about that?

. . . mi, fa, so, la, ti. . . .

Shut up, you, he shouted silently at the ceiling. Just shut up! You don't know what trouble you're causing me. You don't know what I'm doing just to stop from . . . from . . . hurting you. Now just shut up. Just stop that goddamned pounding for a minute, while I find a deck of cards. There must be a deck of cards somewhere around here. Doesn't Tom play cards? Why, sure, everyone plays cards.

He began looking through the apartment, the tic in his face working, his hands trembling, the piano thudding its notes through the floor upstairs, the notes slithering down the long walls of the apartment. When he found the deck in one of the night-table drawers, he ripped it open quickly, not looking at the label, not caring about anything but getting those cards in his hands, wanting only to stare down the king of hearts, wanting to win against the king, knowing if he could defeat the king, his troubles would all be over.

He shuffled the cards and put them face down on the table.

He was trembling uncontrollably now, and he looked up and this time he shouted aloud at the little girl and her piano.

'Shut up! This is important! Can't you shut up a minute?'

The little girl either hadn't heard him, or didn't care to stop practising.

'You little louse,' he whispered. 'I'm doing this all for you, but you don't care, do you? I ought to come up there and just tell you that you stink, that's all, that you'll never play piano anyway, that I could play better piano with one hand tied behind my back, that's what I ought to do. But I'm being good to you. I'm going through all this trouble, trying to beat that red king, and all because of you, and do you give a damn?'

Viciously, he turned over the first card.

A ten of diamonds.

He felt a wave of relief spread over him. Doggedly, he turned the second card. A queen of clubs. Again the relief, but again he plunged on. A nine of hearts. A jack of spades. And then. . . .

The king of hearts.

Upstairs the girl pounded at the piano, the scales dripping down the walls in slimy monotony. The tic in his face was wild now. He stared at the king, and his hands trembled on the table top, and he sought the evil eyes and the leering mouth, and the hidden sword, and he wanted to rush upstairs and stop the piano playing, but, he knew if he could beat the king, if he could only beat the king. . . .

He kept staring at the face of the card.

He did not move from the table. He kept staring at the card and listening to the *do, re, mi, fa* upstairs, and in a few moments, the tic stopped, and he could control his hands, and he felt a wild exultant rush of relief.

I've beat him, he thought, *I've really beat him! He can't harm me any more. That's the last king of hearts! The king is dead!*

And in his exultance, and in his triumph, he began turning over other cards, one after the other, burying the king, hiding him from sight for ever, turning over nines and tens and an ace and a queen and. . . .

The king of hearts.

His heart leaped.

The king of hearts!

But that couldn't . . . no, it couldn't be . . . he'd . . . the king was dead, he had stared it down, beaten it, buried it, but . . .

He stared at the card. It was the king of hearts, no doubt about it, the smirking face and the hidden sword, back again, back to plague him, oh God, oh God there was no escape, no escape at all, he had killed it and now it was back again, staring up at him, staring up with a *do, re, mi, fa.* . . .

'Shut up!' he roared. 'Goddammit, can't you shut up?'

He swept the cards from the table top, the frustrated rage mounting inside him again. He saw the box the cards had come in, and he swept that to the floor, too, not seeing the printed *Pinochle Playing Cards* on its face.

He went to the kitchen with his face ticcing and his hands trembling, listening to the piano upstairs. He took a meat cleaver from the kitchen drawer, and then sadly, resignedly, he went into the hallway and upstairs.

To the Mongol who was playing the piano.

ROBERT SHECKLEY

Will there ever be an end to war? Will mankind, at some time in the future, reach a stage where warfare has become obsolete without making himself obsolete into the bargain? If so, will it be a gradual process or will there have to be a final decisive battle?

According to the Bible, Armageddon, the final battle between good and evil, will be fought at Meggido in Jerusalem and will be followed by the Final Judgement.

Robert Sheckley (1928–) has a well-deserved reputation as a writer of short stories, but he also writes novels. Born in New York, he served with the UN forces in Korea from 1946 to 1948. In *The Battle* Sheckley envisages Armageddon fought in the future between robot armies and the minions of Satan.

13 : THE BATTLE

Sᴜᴘʀᴇᴍᴇ Gᴇɴᴇʀᴀʟ Fᴇᴛᴛᴇʀᴇʀ barked 'At ease!' as he hurried into the command room. Obediently, his three generals stood at ease.

'We haven't much time,' Fetterer said, glancing at his watch. 'We'll go over the plan of battle again.'

He walked to the wall and unrolled a gigantic map of the Sahara Desert.

'According to our best theological information, Satan is going to present his forces at these co-ordinates.' He indicated the place with a blunt forefinger. 'In the front rank there will be the devils, demons, succubi, incubi, and the rest of the ratings. Bael will command the right flank, Buer the left. His Satanic Majesty will hold the centre.'

'Rather medieval,' General Dell murmured.

General Fetterer's aide came in, his face shining and happy with the thought of the Coming.

'Sir,' he said, 'the priest is outside again.'

'Stand to attention, soldier,' Fetterer said sternly. 'There's still a battle to be fought and won.'

'Yes sir,' the aide said, and stood rigidly, some of the joy fading from his face.

'The priest, eh?' Supreme General Fetterer rubbed his fingers together thoughtfully. Even since the Coming, since the kr ledge of the imminent Last Battle, the religious workers of the worl   d made a complete nuisance of themselves. They had stopped thei   kering, which was commendable. But now they were trying to run m   ry business.

'Send him away,' Fetterer said. 'He knows we're pl   ng Armageddon.'

'Yes sir,' the aide said. He saluted sharply, wheele   d marched out.

'To go on,' Supreme General Fetterer said. 'Behind   an's first line of defence will be the resurrected sinners, and various e.   ntal forces of evil. The fallen angels will act as his bomber corps. Del   ceptors will meet them.'

General Dell smiled grimly.

'Upon contact. MacFee's automatic tank corps will proceed towards the centre of the line. MacFee's automatic tank corps will proceed towards the centre,' Fetterer went on, 'supported by General Ongin's robot infantry. Dell will command the H-bombing of the rear, which should be tightly massed. I will thrust with the mechanized cavalry, here and here.'

The aide came back, and stood rigidly at attention. 'Sir,' he said, 'the priest refuses to go. He says he must speak with you.'

Supreme General Fetterer hesitated before saying no. He remembered that this was the Last Battle, and that the religious workers *were* connected with it. He decided to give the man five minutes.

'Show him in,' he said.

The priest wore a plain business suit, to show that he represented no particular religion. His face was tired but determined.

'General,' he said, 'I am a representative of all the religious workers of the world, the priests, rabbis, ministers, mullahs, and all the rest. We beg of you, General, to let us fight in the Lord's battle.'

Supreme General Fetterer drummed his fingers nervously against his side. He wanted to stay on friendly terms with these men. Even he, the Supreme Commander, might need a good word, when all was said and done. . . .

'You can understand my position,' Fetterer said unhappily. 'I'm a general. I have a battle to fight.'

'But it's the Last Battle,' the priest said. 'It should be the people's battle.'

'It is,' Fetterer said. 'It's being fought by their representatives, the military.'

The priest didn't look at all convinced.

Fetterer said, 'You wouldn't want to lose this battle, would you? Have Satan win?'

'Of course not,' the priest murmured.

'Then we can't take chances,' Fetterer said. 'All the governments agreed on that, didn't they? Oh, it would be very nice to fight Armageddon with the mass of humanity. Symbolic, you might say. But could we be certain of victory?'

The priest tried to say something, but Fetterer was talking rapidly.

'How do we know the strength of Satan's forces? We simply *must* put forth our best foot, militarily speaking. And that means the automatic armies, the robot interceptors and tanks, the H bombs.'

The priest looked very unhappy. 'But it isn't *right*,' he said. 'Certainly you can find some place in your plan for *people*?'

Fetterer thought about it, but the request was impossible. The plan of battle was fully developed, beautiful, irresistible. Any introduction of a gross human element would only throw it out of order. No living flesh could stand the noise of that mechanical attack, the energy potentials humming in the air, the all-enveloping fire power. A human being who came within a hundred miles of the front would not live to see the enemy.

'I'm afraid not,' Fetterer said.

'There are some,' the priest said sternly, 'who feel that it was an error to put this in the hands of the military.'

'Sorry,' Fetterer said cheerfully. 'That's defeatist talk. If you don't mind –' He gestured at the door. Wearily, the priest left.

'These civilians,' Fetterer mused. 'Well, gentlemen, are your troops ready?'

'We're ready to fight for Him,' General MacFee said enthusiastically. 'I can vouch for every automatic in my command. Their metal is shining, all relays have been renewed, and the energy reservoirs are fully charged. Sir, they're positively itching for battle!'

General Ongin snapped fully out of his daze. 'The ground troops are ready, sir!'

'Air arm ready,' General Dell said.

'Excellent,' General Fetterer said. 'All other arrangements have been made. Television facilities are available for the total population of the world. No one, rich or poor, will miss the spectacle of the Last Battle.'

'And after the battle –' General Ongin began, and stopped. He looked at Fetterer.

Fetterer frowned deeply. He didn't know what was supposed to happen after the Battle. That part of it was, presumably, in the hands of the religious agencies.

'I suppose there'll be a presentation or something,' he said vaguely.

'You mean we will meet – Him?' General Dell asked.

'Don't really know,' Fetterer said. 'But I should think so. After all – I mean, you know what I mean.'

'But what should we wear?' General MacFee asked, in a sudden panic. 'I mean, what *does* one wear?'

'What do the angels wear?' Fetterer asked Ongin.

'I don't know,' Ongin said.

'Robes, do you think?' General Dell offered.

'No,' Fetterer said sternly. 'We will wear dress uniform, without decorations.'

The generals nodded. It was fitting.

And then it was time.

Gorgeous in their battle array, the legions of Hell advanced over the desert. Hellish pipes skirled, hollow drums pounded, and the great host moved forward.

In a blinding cloud of sand, General MacFee's automatic tanks hurled themselves against the satanic foe. Immediately, Dell's automatic bombers screeched overhead, hurling their bombs on the massed horde of the damned. Fetterer thrust valiantly with his automatic cavalry.

Into this mêlée advanced Ongin's automatic infantry, and metal did what metal could.

The hordes of the damned overflowed the front, ripping apart tanks and robots. Automatic mechanisms died, bravely defending a patch of sand. Dell's bombers were torn from the skies by the fallen angels, led by Marchocias, his griffin's wings beating the air into a tornado.

The thin, battered line of robots held, against gigantic presences that smashed and scattered them, and struck terror into the hearts of television viewers in homes around the world. Like men, like heroes the robots fought, trying to force back the forces of evil.

Astaroth shrieked a command, and Behemoth lumbered forward. Bael, with a wedge of devils behind him, threw a charge at General Fetterer's crumbling left flank. Metal screamed, electrons howled in agony at the impact.

Supreme General Fetterer sweated and trembled, a thousand miles behind the firing line. But steadily, nervelessly, he guided the pushing of buttons and the throwing of levers.

His superb corps didn't disappoint him. Mortally damaged robots swayed to their feet and fought. Smashed, trampled, destroyed by the howling fiends, the robots managed to hold their line. Then the veteran Fifth Corps threw in a counter-attack, and the enemy front was pierced.

A thousand miles behind the firing line, the generals guided the mopping up operations.

'The battle is won,' Supreme General Fetterer whispered, turning away from the television screen. 'I congratulate you, gentlemen.'

The generals smiled wearily.

They looked at each other, then broke into a spontaneous shout. Armageddon was won, and the forces of Satan had been vanquished.

But something was happening on their screens.

'Is that – is that –' General MacFee began, and then couldn't speak.

For The Presence was upon the battlefield, walking among the piles of twisted, shattered metal.

The generals were silent.

The Presence touched a twisted robot.

Upon the smoking desert, the robots began to move. The twisted, scored, fused metals straightened.

The robots stood on their feet again.

'MacFee,' Supreme General Fetterer whispered. 'Try your controls. Make the robots kneel or something.'

The general tried, but his controls were dead.

The bodies of the robots began to rise in the air. Around them were the angels of the Lord, and the robot tanks and soldiers and bombers floated upward, higher and higher.

'He's saving them!' Ongin cried hysterically. 'He's saving the robots!'

'It's a mistake!' Fetterer said. 'Quick. Send a messenger to – no! We will go in person!'

And quickly a ship was commanded, and quickly they sped to the field of battle. But by then it was too late, for Armageddon was over, and the robots gone, and the Lord and his host departed.